HOW TO MAKE A GREAT FIRST IMPRESSION

Pasting on a bright smile for the big Frat party, Cynthia took a step forward, nervously stumbled over her own feet, and plunged headlong toward the floor. She would have fallen flat on her face if a pair of strong arms hadn't rescued her.

"Do you always make a grand entrance like this?" a deep male voice asked.

"Oh, I was just doing my Chevy Chase imitation," Cynthia quipped to cover up her embarrassment.

Still shaken, she looked up to see a handsome boy with dark hair and piercing black eyes staring down at her. He was tall and dressed in total preppy: cords, button-down collar, sport coat, wool tie, loafers and no socks. He was smiling warmly.

Cynthia stiffened, remembering she wasn't supposed to get along with rich kids. Was he laughing at her. . . . ?

CRASH COURSE

BY

Joanna Wharton

A SIGNET VISTA BOOK

NEW AMERICAN LIBRARY

PUBLISHED BY
THE NEW AMERICAN LIBRARY
OF CANADA LIMITED

NAL BOOKS ARE AVAILABLE AT QUANTITY DISCOUNTS WHEN USED TO PROMOTE PRODUCTS OR SERVICES. FOR INFORMATION, PLEASE WRITE TO PREMIUM MARKETING DIVISION, NEW AMERICAN LIBRARY, 1633 BROADWAY, NEW YORK, NEW YORK 10019.

FL 5/IL 8+

First Printing, November, 1985

2 3 4 5 6 7 8 9

SIGNET VISTA TRADEMARK REG. U.S. PAT. OFF. AND FOREIGN COUNTRIES REGISTERED TRADEMARK — MARCA REGISTRADA HECHO EN WINNIPEG, CANADA

SIGNET, SIGNET CLASSIC, MENTOR, PLUME, MERIDIAN AND NAL BOOKS are published in Canada by The New American Library of Canada, Limited, 81 Mack Avenue, Scarborough, Ontario, Canada M1L 1M8

PRINTED IN CANADA
COVER PRINTED IN U.S.A.

Chapter 1

"What a day! I'm lucky to get back here all in one piece."

Agatha Mitchell dumped a mountain of shopping bags onto her bed as Cynthia Woyzek turned from the mirror. "I don't believe these Boston stores, and I don't believe the people. Pushin' and shovin' each other like steers in a feedlot. I put my coat down for one second and a woman wanted to buy it. It's a wonder she didn't yank it right off my back."

Agatha, a tall blonde, collapsed on top of her flowered bedspread. Whenever Agatha was excited or upset, her Texas accent and vocabulary got more pronounced than ever. She sounded like she'd just stepped off the set of "Dallas."

"Shopping can sure be tough." Cynthia knew Agatha would forgive the sarcasm.

"It's a jungle out there." Agatha closed her eyes. "When I'm home, I just run down to Neiman-Marcus, but up here, everything is so exhausting. All these little shops, not

5

to mention Filene's basement, and Boston has so many crazy twisted streets." She sat up suddenly and looked at her watch. "Ohmigosh! What time is the party? I need to steam my face and do my nails."

"Relax. It's not till eight-thirty, and we can always be fashionably late. You even have time to wax your legs." Cynthia tried not to smile. It took Agatha twenty minutes every day just to put on her eye makeup. God knows how long it would take her to get ready for this big fraternity party.

Agatha sank back, relieved. "Then I can sack out for a while," she sighed. She reached for the bottle of witch hazel she kept in her night table. "Sure you don't want to try this?" She doused a couple of cotton pads, lay back, and plopped them over her eyes. "It's simply fantastic for relieving tension. You just have to give it about fifteen minutes."

"I couldn't lie still that long." Cynthia stole another look at herself in the mirror. If only she could manage to look a little foxy just for one night. But shoulder-length brown hair and clear brown eyes weren't going to score any points with the Phi Delts, not when there were knockouts like Agatha around.

"Really?" Agatha murmured. "You know, you're gonna burn yourself out, Cynthia. You're nervous as a cat. Don't you ever feel like just relaxing and letting your mind roll downstream?"

"I don't have the time," Cynthia snapped. "I've got to study for a couple of hours before the party."

"Do it tomorrow," Agatha said drowsily. "Sleep late in the morning and study in the afternoon." She yawned and curled up into a more comfortable position.

"I've got to work tomorrow. They've got me down for lunch and dinner."

"Yuck," Agatha murmured, already drifting off.

Being on a work scholarship was a mixed blessing. Without it, Cynthia never would have had the money to come to Hastings. But secretly she was always afraid it set her apart from the others. There was something humiliating about slinging hash over a steam table while your classmates paraded through the cafeteria line without a care in the world or a thought for the kitchen help.

She picked up her calculus book and moved into the common room so she wouldn't disturb Agatha. She was glad she lived in Windsor Hall, where the dorm rooms were set up as suites. The bedroom had two twin beds with matching night tables, and the common room was outfitted with identical desks and armchairs. Cynthia settled down at her desk and opened her notebook with a sigh.

"Phone call for Woyzek!" Amy Trevlyn stuck her head in the half-open door. In keeping with the latest punk style, she was favoring blue these days. She had just come from the shower with a towel around her head and was dripping blue hair dye all over the hall floor.

"Thanks," Cynthia said, slipping on her shoes. "Hey, is it a guy?" she asked Amy.

"Not unless he sings in a boy's choir," Amy called over her shoulder. Clutching her Japanese kimono around her, she headed back toward the bathroom.

The receiver was dangling where Amy had left it. Cynthia grabbed up the phone.

"Hello?"

"Hi, this is your sister," a familiar voice echoed.

"Oh, Sandi, it's you."

"Don't sound so excited."

"I'm sorry, Sandi. I just sort of hoped it would be someone more on the male side, you know?"

"Yeah, I figured that out." Sandi's tone was dry. "I just wanted to see how your classes were going. You wouldn't get the Nobel Prize for letter writing, you know."

"Hey, I'm sorry. I've just been really busy lately."

"They're not working you too hard, are they?" Sandi persisted.

"No, it's pretty easy, actually." Sandi would know she was lying. But at the moment, Cynthia didn't care. "Say, how are Mom and Dad doing?"

"Oh, everything's about the same," her sister said vaguely. "Dad's still hoping to get back on at the plant, but now they say there won't be any work till spring at the earliest."

"How about you? I don't suppose Neil has a job yet, does he?" Sandi's husband had been laid off from the auto plant a month earlier. Sandi's salary as a beautician barely supported them.

"No, as a matter of fact, he doesn't. He wants to wait to be recalled." Sandi's voice had a ragged edge. "Look, sis, I know this is kind of short notice, but I'm going to be up in Boston in about a week—"

"You're coming to Boston?" Cynthia couldn't keep the amazement out of her voice.

"Yeah, and it would be great if I could see you," Sandi rushed on. "Just pick a place that's easy to find and I'll buy you dinner. I'll be getting in around six."

"But Sandi," Cynthia protested, "what's going on? How come you'll be in town?"

"I'll explain everything when I see you, okay? Just tell me where you can meet me."

"Let's see. The easiest place would be Harry's on North State Street. It's sort of a student hangout—"

"It sounds fine," Sandi interjected. "Look, honey, I've got to run now, but you take care, and I'll give you a call when I get to town. Okay?"

Sandi hung up before Cynthia could say another word.

Cynthia lowered the receiver gently,

trying to fight a mounting feeling of apprehension. What was going on? Had something terrible happened at home?

"What do you mean, Agatha's not ready?" Betty Berke wailed a couple of hours later. "If we get there late, all the hunks will be taken."

"Not to mention the food," Cynthia said.

"I'm too nervous to eat anyway." Pacing the floor, Betty ran her hand through her curly red hair and checked herself out in the mirror. Even though she seemed younger than the other girls in the dorm, she knew how to dress, Cynthia thought, taking in the tan suede skirt and burnished leather boots.

"Agatha shouldn't be much longer. She's doing her Dorian Gray routine."

"What do you mean?" Betty frowned.

"Didn't you read *The Picture of Dorian Gray* in high school? Dorian stays young, but the picture ages—"

Agatha Mitchell burst into the common room dressed in a bra and pants, her beautiful face hidden under a mask of green slime.

"Good Lord, look at you." Betty burst out giggling.

"It tightens the pores," Agatha said calmly. "Has anybody seen my gold earrings?"

"You left them on top of the radiator. *Voila.*" Cynthia handed them to her.

"Thanks very much." Agatha smiled and her fright mask cracked in a dozen places. She waltzed back into the bedroom and shut the door.

"She'll be hours yet," Betty moaned. "Cynthia, why don't you and I go ahead to the party? We'll stop by and pick up Adelle on the way."

"I don't know . . . ." Cynthia always felt uneasy around Adelle Maris; there was something irritating about Adelle's easy confidence. Sometimes she even had the idea that Adelle was laughing at her.

"C'mon," Betty insisted. "We'll see you at the party," she yelled to Agatha, sticking her head through the bedroom doorway. As soon as they were out in the hall, she turned to Cynthia and laughed. "Can you believe it? She's using an electric buffer on her nails. Let's get Adelle and get over there before all the good ones are gone."

Cynthia felt butterflies dancing in her stomach.

"Well, here we are," Adelle said gaily to the smiling upperclassman who took their coats. Cynthia hung back slightly while Adelle and Betty handed over their jackets.

She hesitated and took a deep breath. *Here goes nothing.* Pasting a bright smile on her face, she took a step forward and plunged headlong into space. She would have fallen flat on her face if a pair of strong arms hadn't rescued her.

"Do you always make a grand entrance like this?" a deep male voice said.

Shaken, Cynthia looked up to see a handsome boy with dark hair and piercing black eyes staring down at her. He was tall, maybe six-two, and was smiling warmly.

Mortified, she glanced behind her to see what had happened. She'd missed the shallow step down to the sunken living room. "I was just doing my Chevy Chase imitation," she quipped.

"Hi, Chevy Chase." He held out his hand. "I'm Jim Terkel."

"Cynthia Woyzek." For a moment, her hand lingered in his firm grasp.

"Your nose-dive was very good," he said approvingly. "And I like the purse-throwing routine." He reached under a chair and retrieved her bag. Cynthia had hated the feel of the vinyl since the first time she touched her roommate's leather purse, but apparently her rescuer didn't care. "May I get you a drink?"

"Got any root beer handy?"

"Root beer? What's the matter with *beer* beer?" He looked astonished.

"Pads the hips and rots the liver," Cynthia intoned, smiling up at him. She hated beer and wasn't going to risk harder stuff at this party. She'd probably get drunk and make an ass of herself.

"Root beer—it's eccentric; I'm not sure, but maybe I can scare some up. Otherwise how about a nice cup of tea?"

"Otherwise cola will do. You must have *that*."

He was smiling so warmly that she got embarrassed. For the first time she noticed his clothes and she stiffened, remembering that she didn't get along with rich kids. He was dressed like a total preppy: cords, button-down collar, sport coat, wool tie, loafers, and no socks. He didn't have to settle for polyester and vinyl. He couldn't possibly admire poor little Cynthia Woyzek; he must be laughing at her.

"Excuse me and I'll get your drink." He turned away and disappeared.

I'll bet, she thought resentfully, proceeding to lose herself in the crowd. She didn't want to be left hanging there by herself if he wasn't coming back.

It took Jim a few minutes to find the root beer; it was on the cellar landing with several other "eccentric" soft drinks. He poured a big glass of it with the last of the ice cubes and went in search of Cynthia. He looked for her as long as he could, but a couple of senior brothers chased him back to bar duty.

"Unbelievable," Adelle Maris muttered, watching Jim look for Cynthia with narrowed eyes. "She picks up the best-looking guy in the place and then ditches him."

"What's that?" Betty sipped her drink and made a quick inventory of the room.

Where have the guys been hiding? she thought happily.

"Never mind," Adelle said briefly. She plunked her glass on a coffee table and added sweetly, "Honey, you don't mind if I strike out on my own, do you? After all, we didn't come here to talk to each other."

"That's the truth." Betty laughed. "You go right ahead. I've got my eye on that blond guy in the corner, and I'm just waiting to move in on him."

"Good choice," Adelle said approvingly. She looked at Betty with new respect. *Maybe she's not such an airhead after all.*

The hunk with dark hair had headed toward the kitchen, and Adelle lost no time following him. She pushed her way through the crowd and found him squatting next to a fifty-pound bag of ice.

"If you can get me a refill, you're what I've been looking for all my life," she said sweetly. She gave him a winning smile and held out a plastic glass.

"Coming right up," he said, reaching for a bottle. He let his eyes skim over her, and she was glad that she'd worn her new blue Halston. "Something tells me you're not the type for beer either."

"Right you are." *Either?*

He mixed a gin and tonic and added a twist of lime. "Try that and give me the verdict."

"Perfect. Definitely a ten," she said, eyeing him over the rim of the glass.

"No, I meant the drink," he said solemnly. He was smiling, obviously enjoying the game.

"That too." She grinned. He's just my type, she thought, taking in the lean, rugged face and the thick dark hair that curled around his collar. Cynthia was crazy to let him get away. "How about if we go someplace where we can talk? It's like Grand Central Station in here."

"Sure, but let me fill these ice buckets first. I'm on bartender duty tonight, so I can only be gone for a quick break."

When they squeezed onto an overstuffed sofa a few minutes later, Adelle was annoyed to find that Jim Terkel was one of the most popular boys in the house. She could barely finish a coherent sentence; all his friends kept drifting by for a chat. It was uphill work, but Adelle finally managed to let Jim know that she would love to go out with him sometime. Anytime.

"Have you noticed that they're showing classic films in the Student Center? Everything from Laurel and Hardy to *Casablanca*. Are you interested in that kind of thing?"

"I love old movies," he answered. "I saw *Gone with the Wind* five times, and—" He broke off when Seth Biddle, the fraternity president, tapped him on the shoulder. "I'm afraid duty calls," he said, standing up.

"Maybe we can love them together," she said as he moved away. She thought of following him back to the kitchen and then decided against it. He'd be too busy to talk to her, and anyway, he'd probably call her in the next week or so. She smiled. The evening was shaping up nicely.

Things were going less well for Cynthia, who couldn't seem to strike up a conversation with anyone. She finally spotted Jacqui Orsini, a slender, red-haired girl, who grinned and waved. Cynthia was tempted to wander over and join her, but she hesitated too long and Jacqui was swept away by a tall boy in a blue mohair sweater.

She turned and bumped into someone. "Excuse me," she said, then froze. It was the dark-haired guy she had met before. He'd never shown up with her root beer, she thought resentfully and entirely unfairly. She was convinced he had forgotten.

"We meet again," he said with a big grin. "I knew you couldn't stay away from me. Come to me, my darling, it's destiny."

"What?" Cynthia screeched, outraged. "You're out of your mind, you know that?" But he did have broad shoulders and a smile a person could bask in for days.

He clasped her lightly around the waist and looked soulfully into her eyes. "Have you forgotten? I have your secret craving to satisfy. Just step into the kitchen with me." He regarded her reproachfully. "You've thrown yourself into my arms twice now. Are you toying with me? Trifling with my tenderest feelings?" The hurt look changed to a leer. "Who knows what may happen the third time?"

"You're a creep." Cynthia gave him a push, mortified that he might think she was throwing herself at him.

"Hey, I just meant your root beer—" But she was gone. Jim smiled slowly. He liked them hard to get, and she was harder than he'd seen in a long time.

Not like that clinging, cloying blonde. He wondered if she—Adelle, wasn't it?—was going to be a pest.

Cynthia couldn't wait to get out of there. She was heading toward the coat rack when Agatha Mitchell grabbed her arm.

"I heard him say you were playing hard to get," Agatha drawled. She shook her finger playfully at Cynthia. "Naughty, naughty! I hope you're not turning into a tease."

"You've got to be kidding," Cynthia muttered. "He's a jerk."

"Really?" Agatha's perfectly made up eyes widened in surprise. "He didn't strike me that way at all. In fact, if I weren't happily engaged to Bud, I might have a go at him myself."

"You can have him," Cynthia said, still annoyed. "I wouldn't touch him with a ten-foot pole."

Suddenly the dark-haired boy reappeared, one hand balancing a tray of beer mugs and one glass of root beer.

"It's your friend," Agatha whispered.

"Oh no, not him again," Cynthia moaned. "It's a curse."

He passed by, leaned very close to Cynthia and said, "I didn't get a chance to deliver. Here's your root beer." He thrust the glass into her hand.

She took a step backward from sheer surprise. He winked at Agatha. "She's nuts about me. Can't keep her hands off me. See?" He laughed a little ruefully and moved on.

Cynthia felt like a prize fool. All that yak had been harmless, and she thought—Oh, well. It was too late now. She'd never dare speak to him again.

Agatha giggled. "He's a peach. You really hit the jackpot."

Chapter 2

Betty Berke was racking her brain trying to think of something interesting to say—anything to keep Mitch Goudy at her side. Not that he wasn't easy to talk to. In fact, he was smiling at her in a really friendly way. But sometimes when she was around guys, she froze. Her throat closed up, her mind went blank, and she had difficulty stringing more than two words together.

"Do you like the Phi Delts?" she asked brightly. And immediately thought, What a dumb thing to say. Of course he likes them or he wouldn't have joined.

"They're a great group of guys." He smiled easily. "I think it really helps belonging to a fraternity. Freshman year can be pretty lonely, and it's nice to have a bunch of friends around to show you the ropes."

"But you're not a freshman—"

"No, I'm a junior." He brushed a strand of blond hair out of his eyes. "I joined them—" he looked at the date on his watch

—"two years ago today. I never thought I'd make it through hell week, but somehow I survived in one piece. No visible scars, anyway." He laughed.

You sure did survive. You're perfect, Betty thought.

"How about you?" he went on. "Think you'll be pledging a sorority?"

"I don't think so," she said, then reconsidered. What if he only dated sorority girls? She'd heard that a lot of fraternities and sororities gave parties together. "That is, I haven't really looked into it. It's taken me a couple of weeks just to get settled in. . . ."

"Well, you've got plenty of time," he said vaguely, waving to someone across the room.

Betty was sure he was going to drift away unless she did something fast. "What do you think I should do?" she said in a rush. "After all, you've been here for a couple of years. You must have some ideas on which sororities are good and which ones to avoid."

He sipped his drink and smiled. "I don't know you well enough to know exactly what you're looking for, but I can run down a few of them for you."

"I'd like that," she said promptly. Anything to keep him talking.

Cynthia let her gaze wander around the crowded room as she waited for Agatha to reappear from the ladies' room. She sneaked a look at her watch. She'd stay another half hour and then split, she decided.

She noticed Adelle Maris talking to Jim Terkel. Looking at Cynthia, Adelle smirked and spoke in Jim's ear, her hand on his arm. Cynthia was wondering what poison Adelle was spreading now, when she caught her breath in surprise. Jim gave Adelle a disbelieving look, shook off her hand, and turned his back on her. Adelle gaped after him.

"I don't think we've met." A tenor voice broke in Cynthia's thoughts.

"I beg your pardon?"

"I'm Terence Malley." A good-looking upperclassman in a beige crew-neck sweater was giving her the once-over.

Cynthia looked at him appraisingly, wondering why he had picked her. "I'm Cynthia Woyzek," she said a little reluctantly.

"Freshman?" He raised an eyebrow.

"Yeah. Does it show?"

He laughed. "Not necessarily." He sipped his beer and looked at her thoughtfully.

"How about you?"

"I'm a senior." He paused to assume a worried look. "Does it show?"

Cynthia laughed.

"I bet we have a lot in common," he went on. When she raised her eyebrows, he smiled. "No, it's not a line. I'm a psych major. It's my business to analyze people, to see what makes them tick." He ran his fingers lightly over the palm of her hand. "And I think, deep down, that you and I are kindred spirits."

"Sure. Maybe we knew each other in another lifetime."

He was still holding her hand. "I know one thing about you already. You play the guitar. Classical, I bet." He ran his hand lightly over her fingertips.

"I don't play the guitar. I just like my nails short." She pulled her hand away. She kept her nails short for working in the cafeteria, but she certainly wasn't going to admit that.

"So much for being psychic. You really know how to hurt a guy." He flashed a winning smile to show he wasn't hurt at all. "A Pisces?" he said, pointing to her amethyst birthstone ring.

She laughed. "It's my cousin's. I'm a Virgo."

"Gee, there must be something I can get right. I'm pretty good at accents. I bet you're a midwesterner. I'm going to take a wild shot. Michigan."

"That's right." She smiled.

"Detroit?"

"You've got it. And you're from—"

"Grosse Pointe."

"That's unbelievable," she said, a little warning bell going off in her head. Grosse Pointe was light-years away from her working-class neighborhood in downtown Detroit.

"If you went to Woodhurst Academy, you probably know my sister Andrea," Terence said. "She's a junior there."

"No, I didn't go to Woodhurst," Cynthia said carefully. Woodhurst was one of the most exclusive girls' schools in the country.

"Couldn't stand the uniforms, huh? Grierson Hall, then."

"I went to Wilkins, over on State Street."

"Wilkins?" He dragged it out to a five-syllable word.

Cynthia licked her lips, telling herself to play it cool. "Sure. North Phillips School District."

He laughed nervously. There was a long pause while Terence studied his nails, tasted his beer, and shifted from one foot to the other. Cynthia waited. Then he decided to escape. "Well, it sure has been fun talking to you, Cindy, but I see one of the brothers giving me the sign. Gotta go!" He pretended to nod at someone across the room. "We have to take turns working the bar. Can't even relax at your own party." He forced a dry laugh. "Take care, okay?" He flashed a million-dollar smile and vanished into the crowd.

"Well, scratch number two." Adelle laughed. "Cynthia strikes out again."

"Hmmm?" Susan McMahon said absently.

"Cynthia Woyzek. I've been watching her all evening. She managed to meet two prime hunks and lost both of them. The first is adorable and the second one is rich." Adelle nodded at Terence Malley.

"How do you know?"

"I can smell money from here."

Susan gave a coy smile. "I noticed you were doing a number on that dark-haired hunk earlier."

"Jim Terkel?" Adelle smiled. "Isn't he gorgeous? I think I'm in love."

"C'mon. Get serious." Susan ran her finger around the rim of her glass and licked it thoughtfully. "The salt's the best part of this margarita. I've never had a good drink yet at a frat party."

"Who cares? We didn't come here to drink," Adelle reminded her curtly. "We can do that back in the dorm."

"Well, what did we come for, then?"

Adelle laughed and whispered something in her roommate's ear.

"Adelle, you're outrageous!" Susan drew back, pretending to be shocked.

"I know. Isn't it marvelous?" Adelle sighed and sipped her gin and tonic. It was barely ten o'clock. She'd find someone to dance with, maybe have a few more drinks, and then head back to the dorm. The rest of the evening didn't really matter; after all, she'd already met the best guy there.

And she could hardly wait to see him again.

Cynthia lay quietly in bed, staring at the darkness. What a night! First she made an ass of herself tripping into the arms of Jim Terkel.

Then she got stuck talking to Terence Malley. What a snob, a first-class bastard. If he only knew, it took real brains and guts to get into Hastings from a third-rate school like Wilkins.

Suddenly the room was blindingly bright. "Well, honestly, whatever are you doing sitting here with the lights off?" Agatha Mitchell asked in surprise. She dropped her purse on the bed and took off her earrings.

"I guess I dozed off," Cynthia said hastily, scrambling to sit up. "How come you're back so soon?"

"Oh, I didn't dare stay any later. You know Bud gets crazy if I'm not right by the phone when he calls."

Agatha was engaged to a quarterback at Texas A&M. He called faithfully every night at ten and talked to her for over an hour. How could they find that much to say to each other? Cynthia wondered.

"Hey, have you been crying?" Agatha peered at Cynthia suspiciously. "You look a little misty."

"Crying—who, me?" Cynthia tried to sound tough and confident, but her voice gave her away.

"You weren't upset over that guy who

was teasing you, were you? Jim somebody?"

"Jim Terkel? Hell, no."

Agatha sat down at the edge of the bed. "Well, something must have happened," she said slowly. "I've never seen you like this before." There was a long pause while Cynthia pretended to flip through a fashion magazine. "What did you think of the party?" Agatha asked finally.

"It was a disaster. The worst night of my life." Suddenly she didn't feel like holding back anymore. She told Agatha all about Jim and went on to say what had happened with Terence Malley.

Her roommate's eyes widened. "What a stinking bastard!" Agatha said indignantly. "Don't give him another thought, Cynthia. Luckily, there's only one in a thousand like him—"

"That's not true. What about Adelle Maris and Susan McMahon? They said hi to you tonight and looked right through me, just like I was invisible. Except when Adelle was laughing at me."

"Oh, Cynthia, I'm sure you're wrong about that, just like you were wrong about Jim Terkel," she said placidly. "You thought he was a creep, and he was just making a joke. You should make sure you see him again soon."

"How can I?" Cynthia moaned. "Didn't you hear what he said? That I'm crazy about him? That I can't keep my hands off him?''

"Of course I heard it." Agatha laughed. "I thought it was pretty cute. Probably really means the opposite—he can't keep his off you." She grabbed a bath towel and left Cynthia alone with her thoughts.

A few doors down the hall Betty Berke was tossing and turning, cursing her stupidity. She heard the clock strike eleven and wondered what Mitch Goudy was doing right that minute.

Why hadn't she made more of an effort to hold on to him? Daphne Riesling wouldn't have let him get away, she thought miserably. Daphne knew how to joke and tease, keep a guy interested. Of course, some of Daphne's stories were enough to make you blush, and she was certainly casual about sex . . .

But if a guy really liked you, you shouldn't have to fall all over him to keep him interested.

So what's the big deal? If he likes me, he'll call me. She felt much better and rolled onto her stomach. In a few minutes she was sound asleep.

Adelle slipped between the sheets in a red silk teddy and shivered. What I'd give for a little male companionship, she thought.

Just the thing to warm up a bed on a cold night.

She yanked the pale blue comforter up around her neck and smiled. I wonder if Jim Terkel likes red. Some guys think it's sexier than black. Not that it mattered. She had a whole drawerful of filmy nightwear in all different colors.

She laughed, thinking of the flannel nighties her roommate, Susan McMahon, wore to bed. Susan was so covered, she was practically rape-proof.

You'll never catch me in one of those, Adelle vowed. She had started drifting off to sleep when a thought hit her. Maybe Jim Terkel liked girls who slept in the nude. She decided to ask him the next chance she got.

Chapter 3

For once in her life Adelle Maris couldn't decide on an opening line.

Hi, I was feeling kind of lonely and hoped you were too sounded desperate.

I've been thinking about you ever since the Phi Delt party, and I was wondering if we could get together sometime. Even more desperate.

She was about to settle on *I just wanted to see how you were doing,* when she heard Jim's deep voice and everything flew out of her head.

"Terkel here."

"Jim? This is Adelle Maris," she said cautiously. "We met at a party last week."

"Hi."

Her palms were so sweaty the phone nearly slipped out of her hand. "You were so busy rustling up beers that we hardly got a chance to talk. How have you been?"

A long pause. "I've been okay. Busy. How about you?"

"Oh, same here." That came out in a rush,

and she forced herself to slow down. "You know, lots of classes and projects. Sometimes I look at my crazy schedule and I feel like slitting my wrists. But I guess I don't have to tell you about stuff like that. You're an upperclassman, right?"

"I'm a junior."

"And you're from the south. Georgia."

"South Carolina."

"I was close," she said gaily. He certainly wasn't making this easy. "I love Hilton Head," she gushed. "I used to spend a lot of my summers there."

"I live at the other end of the state."

She almost asked him the name of his hometown and then caught herself. She hadn't called him up to play Twenty Questions. "Well, are the Delts planning any more bashes? I certainly want to get on the guest list. They are one great bunch of guys."

"Nothing's on before Thanksgiving."

"Too bad," she said lightly. "I thought the Delts staged an orgy a month." Dead silence. Wasn't he going to say anything?

" 'Fraid not."

"Well, I'll just have to be patient," she said, trying to keep the whine out of her voice. "Say, how would you like to take a break with me this weekend? Maybe grab a pizza on Saturday night or go to a movie?" She swallowed hard, squinted her eyes shut, and bit her lip. She'd actually asked him out.

"I've got plans," he said easily, "but thanks for the invitation."

"Oh, hey, sure," she said, her face flaming. "It was just a spur-of-the-moment thing. Maybe another time. Gosh, there's quite a lineup here for the phone. Guess I better sign off before I get mobbed. Don't forget to let me know if you hear of any more parties."

"Right, I'll do that. Take care, now." His voice was cool, distant. It was obvious he had no intention of calling her.

"Damn it," she said, slamming the phone into its cradle. She turned and saw Susan McMahon and Jacqui Orsini staring at her. How much had they heard? "Well, you can't win them all," she said, deciding to bluff it.

"That was Terkel, wasn't it?" Susan said shrewdly. "Don't tell me he turned you down."

"He's busy," Adelle muttered. At times Susan could be a giant pain. "So who needs him, right?" She forced a smile. "He's not really my type anyway. I like them tall, dark, and mysterious. Terkel's cute, but basically he's a Georgia cracker."

"I think he's from Harrisburg, South Carolina," Jacqui said helpfully. "That's a little town in the western part of the state."

Adelle's eyes narrowed. Did everyone know more about him than she did? "Well, it amounts to the same thing," she said breezily. She glanced at her watch in mock horror. "Yikes—I've got a French report due tomorrow. I better get over to the library right away or Madame Lacoste will kill me. See you guys later."

"It's funny, I can't imagine Adelle calling up a guy," Jacqui said thoughtfully. "She's so gorgeous I thought she'd have them crawling out of the woodwork."

"Usually she does," Susan said dryly. "But she's hooked—I mean really hooked—on this Jim Terkel. I don't know what the big attraction is, myself. I met him for a few minutes at the Phi Delt party. He's nice, but that's it."

"Maybe it's because he plays hard to get."

"You might be right," Susan admitted. "Adelle is used to calling the shots with guys. So I suppose if Terkel impresses her as someone she can't push around . . ." Her voice trailed off and then she grinned. "Oh, who knows? Nobody can second-guess Adelle."

"Hurry up with the sweet rolls, Cynthia," Mrs. Tyler shouted over the din in the kitchen. "And then take Connie's place behind the counter. I need her to get in here and help me with the pancakes."

"Right," Cynthia muttered, shoving another tray of Danish pastries in the oven.

Business was always brisk on Sundays, probably because the usual breakfast menu was expanded to include homemade breads, waffles, and pancakes. Cynthia took Connie's place and tried not to look at the gigantic mound of creamy yellow scrambled eggs in front of her. She stirred them halfheartedly and unthinkingly slapped a portion onto an empty plate that someone held out to her.

"Hey, I wanted fried," a boy with spiky orange hair griped.

Cynthia smiled. "Sorry." She took the plate, scraped off the scrambled eggs and plopped two fried eggs on a clean plate. "Have a good day," she said, and was rewarded with a scowl.

"Better watch your step, honey, Young Master's in a pet," she muttered to Pamela, who was making toast at the next station. Pamela giggled.

The surly boy overheard and glared at them both. He demanded fresh, hot toast, "Just golden brown, or it won't do," and tapped his foot while Pamela made it. "Is the butter fresh?" he demanded.

"Yes, sir, Your Importance, sir, we churned it this morning at dawn, we did," Cynthia put in.

He gave her a look of outrage and went for coffee.

"My, oh, my," Cynthia squeaked, rolling her eyes. "The service is slow, the food is bad, and the help is uppity. I just don't know what this world is coming to." She made a face.

"Oh, don't pay any attention to him. He's the kind who gives rich people a bad name," Pamela said.

Cynthia stopped dishing up eggs and took a good look at her co-worker. Her uniform was just like Cynthia's, of course, but her earrings looked like real pearls and her shoes like Italian leather. "Come to think of it, you look like you should know. What are you doing on this side of the counter, if you don't mind my asking?"

"I need the money," Pamela said cheerfully, unloading plates from a dishwasher rack. "My parents don't give me an allowance. They say that if I'm old enough to live away from home, I'm old enough to provide my own spending money."

"You mean they could but they won't?" Cynthia asked incredulously.

"That's right. Hey, don't look so shocked. Lots of rich kids work—the cream of the crop if I do say so myself. My parents are a little extreme, but I don't mind. I want to be independent anyway—oh, Lord, look who's coming. Young mistress this time."

Cynthia checked the end of the line and saw Adelle Maris, looking beautiful and bad-tempered. "Gift-wrapped garbage, that one is," she grumbled.

Pamela winked. "Amen, sister."

After work, Cynthia was just leaving the dining hall when she heard some kind of moaning coming from a sofa in the corner of the lounge. It was Susan McMahon. It turned out she had a sick headache that had gotten worse when she smelled breakfast.

"Come back to my room," Cynthia said crisply. "I'll fix you up." Adelle, usually Susan's constant companion, was nowhere to be seen. Cynthia was silently grateful for that. "Listen, if I cure your headache, will you promise to keep it a secret?"

"What?" Susan asked uneasily. "I'm not used to taking pills. What do you have in mind, anyway?"

"Hypnotism. I learned hypnotism from my dentist. I can take care of your headache, but no one else will believe it and I don't want them laughing at me. Got it?"

"You mean you're going to hypnotize me? Now?"

"Only if you want to get rid of your headache."

"How does it work? I've never been hypnotized. That's kind of scary, you know?"

"It's pretty simple, really. We tend to believe what people tell us, especially if they say it enough. Worked great for Hitler —just kidding," Cynthia added hastily at Susan's look of alarm.

"Anyway, the idea is, if I tell you something over and over, you start to believe it. I'll just tell you that you don't have a headache until the idea takes hold and you start to feel better. It's a little more complicated than that, but not much. You'll understand everything that goes on and remember it all afterwards. No tricks, no illusions, no so-called trances. You game?"

"I'll do anything to get rid of this headache. These things may ruin my life."

"You want a posthypnotic suggestion to take them away by yourself?"

"Can you do that?"

"Probably. I can try, anyway. Want me to?"

"Sure. How do we start?"

"Take the armchair. Sit and get settled. If you want a cigarette, have it now so you can free your mind."

"Um, no thanks. Let's just get started."

"Okay. First you have to get relaxed a little. Settle into the corner of the chair so you can rest your head against it if you want to. Lay your arms down. Uncross your legs and let them relax. Do your world-famous imitation of a rag doll. Got it?"

"Okay. What next?"

"You right-handed?"

"Yes."

"Good. Think about your left hand. It feels good, relaxed. The fingers just curl a little. Put your thumb on the tips of your first two fingers. Relax your hand." Cynthia's voice was low and soothing. Already, she could see Susan was beginning to relax. "Now start rubbing the tips of your fingers with your thumb. Good. Make little circles. Keep making them. Think about your thumb and your fingers.

"Feel how good it is to make those little circles? It drains the tension right out of you. Nothing quite so relaxing as making those little circles with your thumb." Cynthia spoke in a low, rhythmic voice.

"Notice how every time you make a little circle, you feel a little better. All those little circles are rubbing your headache away. Every time you make a circle your headache gets a little better. Keep it up. It's helping. You feel a lot better already. You don't feel sick anymore." Most of the tension had now left Susan's face.

"Keep it up. Think about how much it helps. Think about how any time you get a headache, all you have to do is make those little circles and your headache will fade away. You can just rub it away with your thumb and your fingers. Remember, all you have to do is rub your fingers and you won't have a headache anymore. Remember. Keep making circles till you feel like getting up."

Cynthia's voice trailed away and silence fell. She sat still for a few minutes and was thinking about slipping away when Susan stirred.

"It's a miracle! I feel terrific. Now I wish I hadn't missed breakfast. Thanks a million, Cynthia. Wish I could stay and chat, but I blew my schedule away before you came along. Anything I can ever do for you, just let me know."

"Just don't tell anyone."

"Sure. Thanks again."

"Since when are you interested in *The*

Canterbury Tales?" Susan McMahon asked the following Saturday. She was peering over Adelle Maris's shoulder in the library. It was a snowy October morning and her face and hands were red with cold.

"You're dripping snow on my book," Adelle said curtly. She didn't bother turning around to look at her roommate but kept her gaze fixed on the swinging double doors. "I'm waiting for someone." She hoped Susan would take the hint and move on.

"Someone who reads Chaucer?" Susan smirked. "Doesn't sound like your type at all." She flipped the book over and looked at the binding. "You've got a reserved book for English 103. My, my. Some poor bastard is probably looking all over for it, trying to get his assignment done."

"Possibly," Adelle answered briefly. Her heart jumped when she recognized a familiar dark-haired figure coming through the glass doors. Her two-hour wait had paid off. Jim Terkel had come to the library to look up the Chaucer book, just as Leslie Shaeffer had said he would. It was an unbelievable stroke of luck that boring little Leslie was in the same class as Jim and had happened to mention the Chaucer project they were working on.

"Well, I can see you're not going to be any fun today"—Susan pouted—"so I'll have to wade through the Crusades by myself. See you later." She headed for the stacks just as

Jim Terkel reached the reference desk. Adelle watched out of the corner of her eye as he spoke briefly to the librarian and then stared across the room at her. She pretended to be studiously taking notes when a minute later he slid into the seat next to her.

"Adelle? I don't want to be a pest, but the librarian said you were using the Chaucer book Mr. Riggs put on reserve."

"What? Oh yes, I am," Adelle said a little breathlessly. She leaned back in the chair and stretched, knowing that the yellow cashmere sweater accented her figure. "I've been at it all morning," she said, smiling sweetly.

"You're not in my English class, are you?" Jim frowned.

"That's not a very flattering thing to say," Adelle teased him. "Wouldn't you remember if I was?"

"It's a very big class." He smiled and unwrapped his muffler. "You must be in the second section—the one that Udall teaches," he added pleasantly.

"Right." She was beginning to feel a little miffed. Surely she had made *some* impression on him that night at the Phi Delt party. If he weren't so terrific looking, she'd tell him to get lost.

"So what do you think of Udall?" Jim asked. "I've heard he's kind of a nut about iambic pentameter." He leaned close to her and tapped the book thoughtfully. "I think I tend to go along with Riggs's style of criticism. If you concentrate too much on the meter, you lose the whole idea of the beauty of the poem."

He was looking directly into her eyes, waiting for a reply, and Adelle was caught off guard. She'd forgotten what a hunk he was. His shiny black hair was dusted with snowflakes and she could hardly resist the urge to brush them off.

"I . . . uh . . . think Udall gives a very balanced view," she managed to say. She'd have to find a way to swing the conversation away from the stinking book or they'd be sitting here all day. "But I'm such a Chaucer nut, I'm easy to please," she said with a disarming smile. She stretched again and this time was gratified when Jim's eyes slid down her chest. "Even Chaucer can be too much of a good thing, though, don't you think?" She paused. "I'll tell you what . . . it's nearly twelve, so why don't we grab a bite of lunch and compare notes?"

"Well, I don't usually lunch on Saturdays," he began.

"There's always a first time."

"True."

"And I promise to turn this over to you right after lunch." She wrapped her arms around the book protectively.

"I think you've got a deal"—he grinned—"but give me time to go back to the house first, and I'll meet you in the cafeteria at one."

"Great," she told him. "It'll be just the three of us. You, me, and our mutual friend Geoffrey."

He helped with her coat, and she was sure he let his hands linger on her shoulders just a little longer than necessary. Terrific. He was finally getting the message.

Chapter 4

It was eight-thirty and the second floor of Windsor Hall was a tomb. An hour before it had been chaotic—girls everywhere, talking, giggling, dashing in and out of each other's rooms in slips to borrow earrings and curlers, teasing each other about their dates. But now Cynthia felt a familiar ache rise inside her as she made her way slowly to her room.

"Hey, Cynthia, there's a great movie on tonight." She turned to see Leslie Shaeffer sitting in the TV room, a bright smile pasted on her face.

"Thanks, but I better pass. Got to hit the books, you know."

Leslie looked disappointed. "Maybe if you finish early you can watch 'Saturday Night Live.'"

"Sure," Cynthia said easily. "I'll try."

She'd just gotten back to her room when Betty Berke appeared holding a flat cardboard box and grinning. Betty was wearing a pair of black bib overalls with a white turtleneck, and her red hair was a mass of tangled curls. She looked pale, and Cynthia realized it was the first time she'd seen her without makeup.

"Want to pig out?" she offered. There were two Pepsis on the floor beside her.

"Why not?" Cynthia grinned and picked up the drinks. "What's in the box?"

"A large pepperoni-and-mushroom pizza from Amalfi's." Betty opened the box and a pungent aroma filled the room.

"Great." Cynthia laughed. "Let me find a place to put it." She cleared a space on her bed and motioned to Betty to sit down. "I already had dinner, but I can't say no to pizza."

"That's good," Betty said. "Otherwise I'd stuff myself on it. This way I'll just stuff myself on half of it. Daphne got a last-minute dinner invitation and left me stranded." She took a swig of Pepsi and laughed. "She's really cutting it close. She's seeing the first guy for dinner and the second guy for that dance over at the Student Center."

"She has *two* dates for tonight?"

"Yeah, and both the guys are real easy to look at," Betty said. She handed Cynthia a giant wedge of pizza on a paper towel. "You know what she always says about men—if one is good, two are better. She's got guys calling her all the time. She keeps them on the string for a while and then gets bored and moves on. After all, as Daphne says, guys have been doing that for thousands of years, so why shouldn't we women do the same thing?"

"Must be nice," Cynthia said dryly.

"Oh, I don't know about that." Betty was serious. There were two bright spots of color in her pale cheeks. "I think that if you found the right guy, you wouldn't need anyone else, you know?"

"I'm the wrong person to ask about that," Cynthia replied. "My luck at love isn't the greatest."

"Well, I guess mine isn't either—or I wouldn't be spending Saturday night in the dorm."

They ate in companionable silence for a few minutes.

"Did you meet anyone interesting at the Phi Delt party the other night?" Betty asked, licking her fingers. "I saw you leaving early, but I couldn't tell if you were with someone."

"No, I wasn't with anyone. In fact— Well, let's just say I met some guys who were . . . forgettable, that's all."

Betty laughed appreciatively. "Maybe you did better than I did. I met one who was unforgettable."

"And?" Cynthia picked a stray mushroom out of the box and ate it.

"And he never called. His name's Mitch Goudy. Did you meet him?"

Cynthia remembered a tall, good-looking upperclassman who had drifted away from

Betty to talk to someone else. "Yeah, he was nice looking."

"He's a hunk," Betty said passionately. "If he doesn't call soon, I'll go out of my mind."

"Do you expect him to?"

"Well, I hope he will. He didn't take my phone number or anything, but he knows I live in Windsor. And guess who his roommate is? That guy you were talking to, Jim Terkel." She sighed happily. "You know what would really be neat? If the two of us could double-date sometime. Hey, if you see Jim, maybe you could mention it."

"I won't be seeing Jim," Cynthia said flatly. "What do you say we get some more drinks?" She reached for her purse and dug for change. "Just tell me what you want."

"I'll come with you." Betty slid off the bed.

They were on their way to the vending machine when Mary Anne Duffy suddenly appeared at the landing and rushed by them, crying. Her coat was open and her hair was disheveled.

Cynthia and Betty stared at each other for a moment. Betty was the first to react. "Hey, Mary Anne, wait up," she called.

Mary Anne didn't slacken her pace. She dashed blindly down the hall, her high heels clattering on the hardwood floor.

"I wonder what that's all about," Cynthia ventured.

"Let's find out!" Betty started after Mary

Anne. "Did you see her face? Something awful must have happened with her boyfriend." She glanced at her watch and frowned. "It's only ten o'clock. She's never back this early."

Cynthia nodded. Mary Anne usually spent the night with her boyfriend at Boston College.

"I figured something was up when she was alone at that Phi Delt party the other night," Betty continued. "I think it's sweet the way the two of them are always together, don't you?"

"I guess so." Cynthia couldn't imagine why Mary Anne wanted to spend all her time with one boy. She and Bill Rivers went to everything together, hand in hand, like something out of Noah's ark. It was always Mary Anne and Bill, the perfect couple. . . .

When they knocked on her door a few seconds later, Mary Anne was looking composed, but her puffy red eyes were a giveaway. She was clutching a wad of tissues.

"What do you want?" she asked dully, opening the door a crack. Her eyes were ringed with dark circles.

"We, uh, saw you come in," Cynthia began. She looked helplessly at Betty. Maybe they should have left Mary Anne alone. If the situation were reversed, she certainly wouldn't want anyone to catch her crying.

"And we wondered if there was anything we could do," Betty added.

Mary Anne shook her head. "Anything you can do? No, there's nothing you can do." She didn't open the door any wider.

"Wouldn't you like to come down to my room for a few minutes?" Betty offered. "We could get some coffee and talk."

"There's nothing to talk about," Mary Anne said.

"Mary Anne, we know something's wrong. You can't just keep it bottled up inside." Betty's blue eyes were pleading as she reached out and touched Mary Anne gently on the arm.

"I'm going to go to bed now," Mary Anne said in a ragged voice. "I'll see you in the morning. I appreciate your concern, but please—just leave me alone."

"Mary Anne—" The door closed softly. Betty sighed and shook her head. "I hope she's going to be okay. It's something to do with Bill Rivers—I just know it is."

"I'll bet you're right," Cynthia mused. "I wonder what's going on."

But in her mind a strong suspicion was already beginning to form.

Chapter 5

Cynthia had finished her early meal. There was still half an hour before the second shift—enough time for some quick cramming in French.

She'd just opened her book when she heard familiar voices behind her.

"Why are we here so early?" Susan McMahon was asking. "It's not even five o'clock, for heaven's sake."

"I can't *stand* the salad bar when it's been picked over," Adelle Maris explained patiently, watching one of the permanent kitchen workers set out garnishes. "This way we can be first through the line. If we wait, the peasants will demolish it."

Cynthia took a quick look at Susan, then lowered her head over her book. Susan reminded her of a walking Ralph Lauren catalog—gray mohair sweater, nubby tweed blazer with navy pants, leather buttons, Italian loafers.

"Maybe we should just stick to cottage cheese and fruit. Look at that fruit," Adelle whined. "Are we paying through the nose to eat out of a can? I have half a mind to complain to the director of food and housing about this."

Susan whispered something and Cynthia felt two pairs of eyes swing toward her. "Cynthia," Adelle called in her most regal tone, "are you in charge of the salad bar?"

"No!" Couldn't they see she was trying to study? "No."

"Can't you do something anyway?" Adelle rushed on petulantly. "There's no cole slaw or garbanzos."

"No garbanzos? That's terrible," Cynthia said sardonically. "I'll look into it right away." She yawned and went back to her book.

Adelle gave her a withering look and turned to Susan. "Just lazy, I guess," she remarked in an undertone.

Cynthia slammed her book shut and stood up. Karen Jacobs burst in. "Hi, Cynthia, can we join you?" Karen, a bubbly junior from Ann Arbor, was the dorm adviser for Windsor Hall. Jacqui Orsini and Margot Williams were right behind her.

"Sure, sit down," Cynthia said, including Jacqui and Margot in her invitation. The three girls settled themselves with coffee, fruit, and rolls. "No veal cutouts?" Cynthia observed.

"No, thanks. I don't go for cardboard." Margot, a black girl with an Afro, was a vegetarian. At the sight of the veal cutlets, she wrinkled her nose. "Besides, we've got a late-night dinner planned."

"We're taking in a concert in Boston tonight," Karen explained, "and afterwards we're going to Rosemary and Thyme for a late supper."

"I picked the concert," Jacqui said, "Margot found the restaurant, and Karen gets to order for us all."

"Well," Karen smiled at Jacqui—"if you say this string quartet is the best thing to hit Boston this year, I don't want to miss it."

Jacqui flushed. "This group was one of the first I really enjoyed. If it weren't for them, I'd probably be a pianist instead of a violinist. I knew who Yehudi Menuhin was before I could read."

"You're really dedicated," Cynthia said admiringly. She knew what it was like to struggle for something for a long time.

"Sometimes I wonder if it was worth it," Jacqui said, sipping her coffee. There was a hint of sadness in her brown eyes as she looked around the cafeteria. "I always thought I'd end up at Juilliard. . . ." Margot and Karen exchanged a look. It was common knowledge in Windsor Hall that Jacqui considered herself a second-rate musician because she hadn't made it into a top music school.

"The music department here at Hastings does a good job, you know," Karen said softly.

Jacqui gave her a wan smile. "Sure, if you want to teach at a high school somewhere. I always thought I was headed for the concert stage. I used to dream about opening night at Carnegie Hall." She shrugged. "Oh well, what's that line? If I could have been, I would have been . . ."

"You still can, you know." Karen laughed. "You're only eighteen. You've got years to work on your career."

"Tell that to Signore Adamo," Jacqui said ruefully, remembering the fiery scene with her violin teacher that afternoon.

She had been playing a Beethoven sonata —playing so woodenly, in his estimation, that he had snatched the bow out of her hands and threatened to break it.

"*Basta!*" he cried. "You murder the music. You have no style, only technique. You call yourself a musician? Let me tell you something, Jacqui. You have no gift, no heart for music. You do not belong here."

"I've heard he's a tyrant," Karen said sympathetically. "A brilliant musician but not the most patient man in the world."

"He thinks I'm a lost cause," Jacqui said slowly. It seemed impossible. She'd devoted her whole life to music and where had it gotten her? "Sometimes I feel like giving it up completely."

"Jacqui, you can't do that," Karen insisted. "Listen, Signore Adamo"—she lowered her voice—"can be really insulting sometimes. I'm sorry, but you can't let it get to you if he's hurt your feelings. You mustn't throw away a career because of a few setbacks."

"I disagree," Margot put in. "Maybe she's been on one track too long and it's time to head in another direction. Jacqui, when's the last time you did something just for fun? Something that had nothing to do with music? Something crazy and impractical."

Jacqui smiled. "I'm not the crazy, impractical type. You can ask Pete."

"Pete?"

"Pete Adams. He's a guy I met from Stearns Hall a few days ago. A real racing nut. Do you know what he wanted me to do?" She giggled. "Take up car racing! Isn't that insane? He said he'd let me drive his Trans Am. Boy, would he be in for a shock. I almost didn't get my license because of parallel parking."

"You know something?" Margot said slowly. "I think you should reconsider his offer."

"You're kidding!" Karen stared at her.

"Nope. I think Jacqui's ready for a challenge." She looked at Jacqui, her gaze dark and direct. "Am I right?"

"I . . . I'll have to think about it," Jacqui answered. The idea was crazy, and yet she did feel excited just thinking about it. A race-car driver! She started to smile. Maybe there was something in it after all. She'd call Pete tomorrow. There wouldn't be any harm in going to a meet with him.

No one said anything for a moment; then Karen spoke up. "Hey, I've got a great idea. Cynthia, why don't you come with us tonight? I'm sure we can buy an extra ticket at the door."

"No, I have to go to work in a few minutes." Cynthia didn't want to admit that she didn't have the money to go to a concert. "Tell me about this restaurant," she said, hoping to steer the conversation into safer channels. "Is it one of those health-food places?"

"If you mean is everything covered with alfalfa sprouts, the answer's no." Margot grinned. "But they do use all fresh ingredients, lots of herbs, and no meat at all. You're not going to believe this, but my favorite item on the menu is the broiled zucchini burger." She giggled and ran a hand through her curly dark Afro.

"Spare me the details." Karen laughed and held up her hand. "Did you discover this place on your own?"

Margot nodded. "I wandered in one day to buy some pita bread and got into a conversation with the owner. I told him I wrote poetry and he invited me to give a reading that same night. The rest, as they say, is history."

"I'd like to hear your poetry sometime," Cynthia said suddenly. "If you're going to be doing anything on campus, I mean."

"Sure." Margot smiled warmly. "I'm doing a fund-raiser for Save the Whales next month and an antinuke rally sometime around Christmas. I'll make sure I give you the dates."

"Thanks, I'd appreciàte that." Cynthia glanced at the neighboring table and noticed that Adelle Maris and Susan McMahon were staring at her. Was it really so surprising that she could sit down and have a friendly conversation with some of her dorm mates? Maybe she shouldn't have been so quick with the crack about the garbanzos. Adelle and Susan rubbed her the wrong way, but she knew she wasn't entirely blameless. Her mother had often warned her that her quick temper and sarcasm turned a lot of people off.

If only they knew me better, she caught herself thinking, maybe they'd realize that sometimes I blurt out things without thinking—and that most of the time it's because I feel so scared and insecure. . . .

She would have felt even worse if she had known what they were really saying.

"Stop fidgeting, will you?" Adelle snapped. "You do that all the time these days. What's the matter with you?" Susan was rubbing her fingers together the way Cynthia had shown her. Studying. So far only Adelle had noticed, but she wouldn't shut up about it.

"Er, it—it makes my head feel better. I've been living on No-Doz during midterms, and my head is ready to explode."

"So take an aspirin, but cut that out."

"Oh, all right, I'll try."

But a minute later Adelle was again on her case.

"I'm telling you, Adelle, it really makes my head feel better. Do you want me to have a headache?"

Before she knew it, Susan was telling Adelle all about her sick headache and Cynthia's hypnotism.

"Honest, Adelle, it was amazing. She just sat me down and talked to me for a while. She had me rub my thumb and fingers together like this and pretty soon it was like I never heard of a headache."

"Don't be ridiculous, Susan. You were getting over it anyway. Hypnotism is a crock." Adelle glared across the room at Cynthia, who had her table mates in stitches over a story she was telling.

"Well, maybe."

"I'll prove it to you. I'll get her to try to hypnotize me and we'll see what happens."

"Don't do that, Adelle. I promised I wouldn't tell anyone. She doesn't want to be asked to do it."

"Well, you broke your promise, didn't you? Serves you right if she gets mad at you." Adelle got up and marched over to Cynthia's table. "What is this I hear about you making a fool of my roommate?"

Cynthia had just finished her story and the girls at her table were still laughing. She looked up blankly. "Huh?"

"What's this about you pretending to

cure headaches? You'd better leave my roommate alone with that crap."

"What are you, jealous?" Cynthia smiled affably at Adelle, then glanced at Susan, who was watching miserably from her seat at Adelle's table. Cringing a little, Susan got up and made herself walk over to Cynthia's table.

Adelle flushed dull red. It was true; she thought of Susan as her personal property. That was what made her so mad; to hear her own roommate, her sidekick, praising the enemy. "Not hardly," she sneered. "I just don't like to hear of a decent girl being taken advantage of."

"Now, I wonder what I did to hurt her," Cynthia mused aloud. "Did I make her headache worse? No, that can't be it. Did I ask her for money or anything? Don't remember doing that. Did I spread her secrets around campus?" She cocked an eye at Susan, who was hovering uncertainly at Adelle's elbow.

"Cynthia, I—"

"Never mind, Sue," Cynthia interrupted soothingly. "It's okay. It was just a sideshow trick anyway." She smiled gently. "I know how it is. You lackeys have to follow orders. If you didn't carry stories and brown-nose Adelle, she wouldn't like you anymore. Wouldn't that be awful, to lose the friendship of such a wonderful person just to keep a solemn promise to someone like me?"

"Promise, my eye," Adelle snapped. "You just didn't want anyone to find out what a fake you are." She was getting loud, and several kids who were just finishing their meal stopped to see what was going on. Mitch Goudy was one of them; he was having lunch with a pledge.

"Fake, is it? Look who's talking—you know all about it, don't you? Fake eyelashes, fake fingernails; I'll bet your nose is fake, too," Cynthia jeered.

"You leave my nose out of this," Adelle yelped. She had gotten a nose job for her high school graduation present.

Cynthia grinned evilly. She knew when she had hit a sore spot. "I'd love to, but you already stuck it in. You want me to leave your nosy little nose alone? Then say you're sorry you called me a fake."

"I will not! You're a fake and a liar besides." Adelle had become shrill. "You can't do hypnotism. You tried to put one over on Susan, and I resent it."

Cynthia decided to see how far she could push Adelle. "Now just a minute," she drawled. "I hypnotized Susan and I bet I can do it to you too."

"Not likely. I'd probably throw up from listening to you."

"See that?" Cynthia announced to a fascinated audience. "She's afraid to put her money where her mouth is. Tell you what, Adelle. I won't even take your money—

wouldn't be fair to bet on a sure thing. I'll just challenge you."

"What do you mean, challenge me? That's a laugh."

"You called me a liar; I want to prove I'm not."

Adelle didn't like the sound of that at all. "Now, wait a minute, Cynthia—"

"Wait for what? Either I can do it or I can't. If I can, I deserve to prove it; if I can't, you'll have the last laugh." Cynthia turned to the crowd that had gathered. At least a dozen students had stopped to listen on their way out. And the entire cafeteria staff was gathered around Cynthia. "Is there any point in waiting?"

"Sure isn't," called Pamela, the girl who worked on the serving line with Cynthia.

"Don't see any," someone else said.

"Just a minute, here," Adelle faltered.

Cynthia saw that Adelle was on the defensive; pressing the advantage, she spoke loudly to the audience again. "I say that I can hypnotize Adelle Maris so her nose will itch all day, and I say, further, that if she refuses, she proves she's a liar and a coward."

"Right on!"

"Show us how it's done!"

"Come on, Adelle, you can't say no to that."

Trapped, Adelle submitted ungraciously. "Oh, all right. Go ahead and try. But do we have to do it here? Let's go back to my room."

"No way!"

"We get to watch!"

"Sit down and get started, will you? I have a class in half an hour," Mitch Goudy's pledge put in.

Cynthia glanced over and noticed Mitch for the first time. "Hey, Mitch, sit down here a minute, will you please?" She pulled out a chair for him.

"Sure, Cynthia. Anything to oblige. What do you want me to do?"

"You're the magician's assistant from the audience; all you have to do is sit there and look gorgeous. It's this—er—*lady* who gets sawed in half." She smiled falsely at Adelle and set another chair a couple of feet away, facing Mitch's. "Do please sit down, my pretty," she cackled, rubbing her hands together.

Adelle cast her eyes to heaven as if in prayer and slouched in the chair. "That's perfect." Cynthia nodded. "Just take it easy and get comfortable."

She turned to the audience. "You're welcome to watch, but I do need silence. Why don't you all sit down?" She waited till everyone had taken a chair before she spoke again. "Please note the alligator emblem on my assistant's sweater. Everyone look at the alligator. Look at the alligator. Don't take your eyes off the alligator, and don't make a sound. You don't want to talk anyway. You like to be quiet and look at the alligator. Keep quiet and watch the alligator. Nobody wants to talk. Just look at the alligator."

A curly-haired freshman girl giggled and was fiercely hushed. After that you could have heard a pin drop.

"Adelle. Don't look at me. Just look at the alligator. Now think about your nose. Look at the alligator and think about your nose. The alligator is making your nose itch. It's staring at your nose and making it itch."

Adelle's hand started for her face.

"No, don't do that. You can't scratch it yet. It doesn't itch quite enough yet for you to scratch it. Just lay your hand down. Lay your hand in your lap and look at the alligator. Soon your nose will really itch badly, and you have to save your scratching for then."

Suddenly Adelle shook her head and started to stand up. "See?" she sneered. "It doesn't work."

"Give it a chance," someone called. "You have to let her finish or it doesn't count."

"Yeah, sit down," Mitch said. "Unless you want everyone to say you chickened out."

Adelle sighed heavily and sat down again. She started to raise her hand toward her face, then jerked it back into her lap. "All right, get it over with. I don't have all day."

It didn't take long to get the audience

quieted down. Everyone was concentrating on Mitch's alligator. In a minute or so, Cynthia was ready to take up where she had left off.

"The alligator is making your nose itch. Your nose is going to itch a lot for the next week, but it will get worse when you see an alligator. All alligators make your nose itch.

"Now the inside of your nose itches too. The whole thing itches like crazy—up between your eyes, down around the nostrils. You have the itchiest nose in the world. But the awful part is the inside. That itches the worst, and it's the alligator that's doing it.

"Now, go on. Scratch your nose. Do it good and hard; use your fingernails. That's right, scratch. See how your nose still itches? Scratching it doesn't do any good, but you have to try anyway.

"Keep it up. Keep looking . . . Keep scratching . . . Look at the alligator. . . ."

At last Cynthia's voice faded away. "Okay," she said briskly after a pause, "everyone look at Adelle."

Her face was red and contorted. She was screwing up her cheeks to try to get at the itch inside. Her nose was red and blotchy from scratching and rubbing. She had her fists clenched in her lap and was stealing furtive looks at Mitch Goudy's sweater. Everyone howled with laughter.

Adelle turned to the watchers and saw a

solid rank of five kids with Izod shirts or sweaters standing there shoulder to shoulder and grinning at her. She burst into tears and ran from the cafeteria.

Chapter 6

Late that afternoon Mitch Goudy walked into the living room of the Phi Delt house and found Jim Terkel dozing on a big leather sofa with an economics textbook on his chest. "Say, my man, this is the wrong time of day and the wrong place for that," Mitch remarked.

"Only thing wrong with it is that nobody will leave you alone," Jim grumbled.

"See what I mean? Wrong time, wrong place."

"Yeah, well, I gotta read this assignment anyway. Put me right to sleep, it did. By the way, where were you at lunch? We have thirty-six alumni brothers coming for this weekend's football game, and they all want to stay here. Gonna have trouble finding places to put them. I said you'd bunk in with me and let them have your room."

"Why me?"

Jim grinned. "That'll teach you to make your bed in the mornings. You won the prize for most-presentable bedroom."

"Hey, thanks." Mitch started toward his room then stopped. "Say, you'll never guess what just happened in the dining hall. The damnedest thing!"

"Do tell."

"You know Adelle Maris?"

Jim groaned. "Oh, yeah. Nobody's lucky all the time."

"Wait, you're going to love this story. She picked a fight with Cynthia Woyzek, right there in the cafeteria."

Jim sat up straight. "Bad news for Cynthia, I guess. Adelle Maris is nobody to mess with."

"Not to worry, my friend. Cynthia sent her running off in tears."

"Wish I could do that. How'd it happen?"

Mitch laughed. "Wait'll I get us a couple of beers. Can't do justice to this one on a dry throat."

Returning with two Buds, Mitch made himself comfortable in an easy chair and launched into a highly colorful account of Cynthia's performance. By the time he got to the part about everyone in an Izod shirt lining up in front of Adelle, Jim was laughing so hard he was nearly crying.

"Oh, Lordy." Jim chuckled. "I wonder how many clean alligators I have in the closet. We should all wear them for about a week. . . . You know, I really liked Cynthia, but I didn't call her up because it didn't seem to be too mutual. Maybe I'll try again.

Anybody who can do that to Adelle Maris is worth cultivating."

A couple of days later, Cynthia was slaving over her calculus homework when Agatha Mitchell burst into the room, all smiles. She was in a wonderful mood—probably because she'd been shopping, Cynthia noted wryly—and happily dumped a mountain of packages on her bed.

"It has been the most fantastic day!" she said, shrugging off her fur-lined raincoat. Running a brush through her shimmering blond hair, she grinned at Cynthia. "What have you been doing all afternoon?" She frowned at the book. "Working again!" she said in mock reproach. "Haven't you heard the expression 'all work and no play'? You know what happens to people who do that, don't you?"

"Sure. They pay their bills on time."

"Nope." Agatha laughed, "It makes them dull. D-U-L-L." She flipped the calculus book closed. "That's enough of *that* for one day."

"Hey!" Cynthia protested. "I've only got an hour to study before I go to work."

Agatha kicked off her high heels and sat cross-legged on her bed. "Fortunately, today's your lucky day, Cynthia. Today I've got a little surprise for you. Actually, two surprises." Agatha, looking enormously pleased with herself, grinned at her roommate.

"Well, don't keep me in suspense." There was no point trying to study when Agatha was in one of her talkative moods.

"Well, here goes! You, Cynthia Woyzek, have just won a date with one of the nicest, cutest guys in the world."

"Very funny. You should be doing Carson." Cynthia reached for her math book.

"No, hey, I mean it!" Agatha snatched the book away. "Will you listen to me—you've got a date with a really neat guy. A super guy, honest! And I'm not going to give the book back until you say you accept."

Cynthia made a swipe at the book, but Agatha was too quick: she held it over her head.

"Cynthia Woyzek, you're the stubbornest person I've ever met. What do I have to do to convince you?" Agatha wailed. "Here I went to all the trouble to set it up for you—"

"Trouble?" Cynthia queried in a dangerous voice.

"Wait, I didn't mean that the way it sounded." Agatha laughed nervously. "Actually, it was no trouble at all. It was sort of fun. It's always fun to be a match-maker, you know."

"Agatha," Cynthia growled, "tell me what you did. Exactly."

Agatha swung her long legs off the bed and began opening her packages. "I, uh, got you a blind date." She kept her back turned to Cynthia as she pulled out a pair of black velvet jeans. "What do you think of these? Are they too much? I don't want to end up looking like Amy Trevlyn," she said, referring to Windsor Hall's resident punker.

"You did what?" It was Cynthia's turn to slam the book shut. "You've got nerve. You got me a blind date without even asking me? What made you think I'd go?"

"Well, of course you'll go," Agatha said smoothly. "Of course I would've asked you, but there wasn't time. You know what my daddy always says: 'When you see an opportunity, grab it—or someone else will.' "

Cynthia sighed. Agatha's father, one of the wealthiest men in Dallas, had an apparently inexhaustible supply of sayings.

"You're really doing me a big favor, you know," Agatha continued.

"How's that?"

"This date—he's Bud's best friend. When Bud told me Jerry was coming to Hastings for the weekend, I told him I'd get a date with the nicest girl I knew. And that's you," she said triumphantly. "You'll love Jerry. He's just your type."

"Agatha, read my lips," Cynthia said. "I'm not going on a blind date with Bud's friend—or with anyone else. In the first place, I never go on blind dates—"

"Then it's time you started," Agatha said crisply.

"In the second place," Cynthia went on quickly, "I've got nothing to wear." She had no intention of showing up in that brown polyester dress again—ever.

"Wrong, wrong, wrong!" Agatha crowed. "Look, you do have something to wear. That's surprise number two." She tossed Cynthia a gold foil shopping bag from one of Boston's most exclusive shops.

"What's this?" Cynthia gingerly opened the bag and pulled out one of the most beautiful sweaters she'd ever seen. It was cream-colored angora with a high Victorian collar and long sleeves. She held it up against her, running her fingers over the tiny satin ribbons that were beaded through the bodice.

"It fits you perfectly, I knew it," Agatha exclaimed. "You can wear it with your black wool skirt."

Cynthia carefully folded the sweater and put it back in the bag. "I can't take this. I don't like to borrow from people."

"Oh, it's not a loan." Agatha laughed. "It's . . . a little present. It's yours."

"A present?" Cynthia demanded incredulously. "You know I can't take anything like that."

"Listen, Cynthia, they were having a one-cent sale at Chalmers. Buy one sweater at regular price, get another for a penny. I bought that black sweater for myself, so yours only cost a cent. I can't return it and it doesn't fit me, so you're stuck with it."

"Agatha, I wish you hadn't," Cynthia protested. "How can I thank you?"

"Say you'll go out with Bud's friend. I told him what a really super girl you are, and I just know the two of you will hit it off."

"When did you say it was?" Cynthia asked, weakening.

"This Saturday night at seven o'clock. For dinner."

"I have no choice?"

"You have no choice. It's all arranged. As Daddy says, if you're going to do something, do it right."

On Saturday night, Cynthia was in her room, trying on one outfit after another while Betty Berke offered encouragement.

"It's beautiful," Betty said enviously, running her hand lightly over the rich angora. "The thing is, how do you know what to wear if you don't know where you're going?"

"Good question." Cynthia slid the sweater over her head and frowned. A one-cent sale at Chalmers? Well, maybe.

"God knows what kind of guy Agatha's found for me." Cynthia shook her head. "All I know is that he's from Texas."

"Texas? It sounds so romantic!"

"What's so romantic about dating a Texan?"

"Oh, I don't know," Betty mused. "Maybe he's an oil baron or a rodeo king."

"I don't think so," Cynthia said firmly. "He goes to school with Agatha's fiance."

"A Texas preppy?"

"Yup. He probably wears a ten-gallon hat with an alligator on it. Or maybe he goes whole hog and keeps his alligator on a leash."

They were still laughing when Cynthia heard a shout from the other end of the hall.

"Woyzek—there's a phone call for you!"

Cynthia slipped on her shoes. She knew what that call was. Jerry was calling to say he couldn't make it. It figured.

"I'll only be a minute," she said to Betty. "Do you want to wait for me?"

"No, I've got to split." Betty scrambled off the bed. "I told Daphne I'd French-braid her hair tonight." She picked up a bag of Oreos and headed for the door.

The receiver was lying on the shelf.

"Hello?"

"Hi, sis."

"Sandi!"

"You sound so relieved—"

"Well, yeah, actually." Cynthia laughed. "I was supposed to have a blind date tonight, and I thought it might be the guy, whoever it is, calling to break it."

"Nope. Only your sister. But I'll be there tomorrow night. Can you meet me at that place—"

"Harry's? Sure."

"North State Street?"

"Yeah, can you find it?"

"Of course. About seven o'clock all right?"

"That's fine."

There was a moment's pause. "It'll be great to see you, sis."

"Same here, Sandi."

"Well, so long." There was a click at the other end of line.

Cynthia felt the old wave of concern sweep over her. Why was it that everything connected with her family had to be so complicated? She knew there was something wrong. Sandi wouldn't be flying to Boston for a weekend spree. She couldn't afford it, for one thing.

Well, tomorrow night was soon enough to find out. And secretly, Cynthia was very very glad that it wasn't *tonight* her sister was arriving.

"Daphne, what would you do if you wanted a boy to notice you?" As soon as the words were out of her mouth, Betty Berke realized how silly they sounded. What boy wouldn't notice Daphne Riesling? She was a knockout.

Daphne smiled tolerantly at her roommate and took a long drag on her cigarette. "Who do you have in mind, sweetie?"

"Oh, just someone I met," Betty said vaguely. Her fingers worked quickly as she twisted Daphne's long hair into gleaming plaits.

"The guy you met at the Phi Delt party?" Daphne asked shrewdly.

Betty blushed furiously. "Did I . . . mention him to you?"

"You didn't have to." Daphne wriggled away from Betty's grasp long enough to color her mouth with strawberry lip gloss. Tony Robbins should have fun chewing that off, she thought happily. "I saw you talking to him the night of the party. It looked like instant chemistry between you. Am I right?"

Betty nodded. "I can't stop thinking about him. I suppose it sounds crazy to someone like you. You can have anyone you want."

"Not really," Daphne drawled. "Well, *almost* anybody."

"How do you do it?" Betty blurted out. "I mean, it's more than looks, isn't it?"

"It's all in the mind, sugar." She stubbed out her cigarette and carefully inspected her pearly-white teeth.

"What do you mean?" Betty put down the comb.

"Oh, you know. It's the whole package— the way you walk and talk, the signals you send out," Daphne said vaguely. She picked up the comb and handed it to Betty.

"Do you think I could learn it?"

Daphne looked Betty over. "I don't think so. I mean, it's not in any book or anything." Daphne shrugged and eased her diamond posts into her lobes. "Look, you're great just the way you are, Betty. It would be a mistake to try to imitate somebody else." She stared at Betty's crazy T-shirt and baggy painter's overalls. "You've got your own style, and that's what you've got to cultivate."

Daphne knew that sounded familiar, and then she remembered. She had just read it in *Cosmopolitan.*

"I guess you're right," Betty sighed. "I don't think I could be anything else even if I tried."

"That's the spirit," Daphne said warmly. "If this guy doesn't like you the way you are, then who needs him, right?"

"Right." Now if only there were some way to make herself believe it.

"Uh, Betty, I don't want to be a drag, but do you think you could hurry just a tiny bit?" Daphne flashed a bright smile. "You should never keep them waiting too long. I remember once . . ."

Betty finished Daphne's hair while Daphne told her the impatient-date story.

After Sandi's call, Cynthia settled down for an hour's studying before her date. But it was impossible to study. She found herself staring blankly at her calculus book, wondering what was going on at home. Why in the world was Sandi coming to Boston?

By seven-thirty she was running hopelessly late. Her hair dryer blew out and

Cynthia had to borrow Agatha's high-powered contraption that whined like a broken air conditioner.

"Cynthia, your date's here," Leslie Shaeffer shouted from the doorway.

Cynthia switched off the dryer and glanced at her watch. The mystery date was right on time. "Okay, thanks. I'll be down in a minute."

After a pause, Cynthia realized that Leslie was still standing in the doorway. "Got a big night planned?" she asked.

Cynthia shrugged. "Blind date. Dinner in Boston and maybe a movie, I guess. He's a friend of Agatha's quarterback."

"Really?" Leslie sounded impressed. "Well, he's super good-looking. He's tall with dark hair and eyes, and he's got on this really neat sport coat with a sweater—supreme preppy."

"That's all I need," Cynthia muttered. She took a final look in the mirror and decided she'd pass. The angora sweater looked terrific.

"Have fun," Leslie said a little sadly. She had a notebook tucked under her arm and was obviously going to spend another long night in the dorm.

"I'll try."

Cynthia stared in disbelief at the boy who was standing in the lounge. His smile was dazzling.

It was Jim Terkel.

"You look great!" Jim beamed at her. "Hope you like seafood. I found this terrific place right on the waterfront. Best fried shrimp in town. Of course, they have lobster and steak too, but the shrimp is the best. They use beer in the batter."

Cynthia opened her mouth to reply, but Jim didn't give her a chance. Lifting the coat from her arm, he held it out for her. "Better bundle up; it's chilly out." He smiled. He pulled up the collar of his camel-hair coat and tossed a white scarf around his neck.

Cynthia had almost forgotten how sensational he looked—rugged features, thick black hair, and the darkest eyes she'd ever seen.

Before she knew it, Cynthia was out on the porch in the chill night, surrounded by other departing couples. She caught sight of a dark green van.

"I've been set up and shanghaied," she muttered darkly as he opened the van door for her. She knew what she'd do—turn the tables. She'd let him buy her the best of everything and then turn her tongue loose and cut him to ribbons. As for Agatha, for two cents Cynthia would melt down all fifteen of her roommate's expensive lipsticks into her expensive shoes and pour them on her expensive hair.

As soon as they were out of the wind, she turned to Jim and demanded, "Okay, Jerry-Jim, tell me what this is all about."

He grinned. "It's simple. Mitch and I were talking and your name came up. I remembered you from the party and said I'd like to take you out. Then I ran into Agatha, and she offered to play matchmaker. Did she actually tell you my name was Jerry?"

"She certainly did. Otherwise I—"

"Otherwise what?" Jim started the van.

"Nothing. She said you were a friend of her boyfriend from Texas A&M."

"That's Agatha for you." He looked over his shoulder and pulled out. "She loves surprises. Loves to do a favor too. Gives her a glow. It's one of the nicest things about her." Jim glanced over at Cynthia, a smile playing around his lips. "I hear you do hypnotism. Want to hypnotize me?"

"What?" she screamed.

"Mitch told me. That's how your name came up. It's all over campus by now."

"This is too much. No, I do not want to hypnotize you. I want to drop the subject— permanently."

"Yes, ma'am. Say, you look a little chilled. Maybe you should move over closer."

Cynthia folded her arms. "What an original idea!"

Jim kept up a running commentary all the way to the waterfront, pointing out historical sights. "That's the opera house on the left and Lafayette Place on the right, except it's too dark to get a very good look," he said cheerfully. "Once we get on State

Street, it will take us all the way out to Atlantic Avenue and we'll be right on the wharf."

"Terrific," Cynthia looked at Jim again. He was smiling, handsome, without a care in the world, and apparently determined to show her a good time. In fact, he was pretty hard to resist.

Chapter 7

"It's nice, isn't it?" Jim said with a grin. He'd wangled a candlelit table by the long bay window, which commanded a breathtaking view of Boston Harbor. Outlined in twinkling lights, a barge drifted slowly through the inky waters. He watched it for a moment before turning his attention back to Cynthia. "This is one of my favorite restaurants in Boston," he added contentedly.

Cynthia rewarded him with a thin smile. She'd felt awed from the moment they stepped into The Landing, and it was a constant battle not to show her surprise. Wait till she told Sandi about this tomorrow! She glanced around the elegant room, taking in the snowy tablecloths, the silver wine coolers, the heavy crystal water goblets, trying to imprint every detail on her memory. When Jim had suggested a seafood restaurant, she'd pictured a neighborhood bar and grill like Danny's back in Detroit—some place with red vinyl seats and fishnets for decoration. Cynthia reached out and touched one of the fresh white carnations arranged in a small pewter bowl.

"What would you like for an appetizer?" Jim asked.

Cynthia turned her attention to the menu. "Well, I don't know," she mused. "Do you suppose they serve fish?"

Adelle Maris and Randy Owens were sitting in a dark corner of the Student Center lounge.

"I think I met one of your frat brothers a few weeks ago." Adelle tried to make her voice sound casual. "Jim Terkel?"

"Oh, yeah, Jimbo," her date replied. "Great guy." He peered at her suspiciously. "Are you dating him or something?"

"Oh heavens, no." Adelle laughed easily. "We have mutual friends, that's all, and I wanted to look him up. Anyway," she said, trying unsuccessfully to drag his attention away from her plunging neckline, "do you know Jim very well? I barely had a chance to talk to him at the Phi Delt party, so I don't really know what he's like."

She smiled brightly, hoping she could penetrate Randy's foggy brain. He shifted his stare to her lips and she wanted to scream. What was she doing out with this creep? She should be with Jim Terkel.

"Jim's an okay guy." He spoke slowly, as if it cost him a great effort. Obviously,

Randy Owens had decided that the time had come to make his move. "How come we're talking about him when we could be talking about us?"

It was the longest sentence he had strung together all evening, and Adelle felt encouraged. "I'm just curious, that's all," she said. His hand was making steady progress down her neckline, and she grabbed it firmly.

"What's wrong?" he muttered.

"Do you know what clubs he's in, what classes he takes?" she persisted. "Is he dating anybody? Does he have a steady?"

"Who?" he said huskily. The hand began its inexorable progress again.

"Jim Terkel," she whispered. "Don't you know anything about him?"

Randy suddenly bent down and crushed her mouth in a sloppy kiss. "All I know is, you're one sexy broad, Adelle."

"Home at nine-thirty?" Susan McMahon looked up in amazement. "Randy must not have lived up to his name." Clad in a pair of red-and-white ski pajamas, Susan turned down the television and grinned at her roommate.

"He was impossible." Adelle poured herself a glass of wine and started removing her makeup.

"Wildly sexy?"

"Wildly creepy. He practically tried to

rape me on the couch at the Student Center. The janitor came by just in time. Then he tried to lure me back to his room, but I told him I had a splitting headache."

"Naughty, naughty."

"It's not far off the truth."

"What's so awful about him?"

"He's a Phi Delt," Adelle said shortly. She glanced in the mirror. She looked like someone who'd just been to a wrestling match. "And I—I wanted to find out something about one of his fraternity brothers."

"You're still hung up on Terkel," Susan accused her. "I knew it." She helped herself to a glass of wine. "Is this guy going to set you up with him or something?"

"No, I hit him over the head with the idea all night, but he didn't take the hint."

"I thought you had lunch with Jim in the cafeteria," Susan said.

"Nothing came of it. I'm going to lure him back for lunch again with some questions about Chaucer."

"The guy plays hard to get."

"He sure does. But I'll get him."

Susan looked at her roommate slyly. They had lived together for three months and had tagged each other five minutes after they met. She smiled and took a sip of Chablis. "I'll bet you will," she murmured.

"What shall we drink to?" Jim hesitated before touching his glass to Cynthia's.

Their appetizers had just come. He had ordered oysters for himself, and a pate for her, and a wine she'd never heard of.

"To your sign," Cynthia said promptly.

"Scorpio?"

"Alligator. I figure you were probably born with one on your chest."

"That's right. I had to wrestle it for my silver spoon."

"You're lucky you won."

"I cheated. Hypnotized the beast. Want me to show you?"

"Drop it, Jim. Your true colors are showing." She took another sip of asti spumante and was pleased at the warm feeling that coursed through her. One of the advantages of being a wealthy preppy, she decided, was that you could afford good wine.

"Got me all figured out, have you?"

"Sure do," Cynthia said pleasantly. She looked at him appraisingly. "College sophomore . . . Phi Delt . . . probably majoring in business or marketing . . . wealthy East Coast family . . . fat clothing allowance . . . never worked a day in your life." She watched his face for some sign, but his dark eyes were impassive. "Stop me if I'm wrong."

Jim burst out laughing. "You're wrong on all counts . . . The only thing you got right was the fraternity." He paused and nibbled on a roll. "I'm a junior and an English major, and I'm not as much of a playboy as you seem to think. Ever since I was sixteen I've spent my summers working for Dad's company—he owns a small firm in South Carolina that distributes computers and software."

Embarrassed, Cynthia dropped her eyes to her plate. The mysterious pate looked for all the world like Aunt Helen's chopped liver. "Public relations or personnel?" She tasted it. It *was* chopped liver—good, too.

"Neither. I worked in shipping and receiving—otherwise known as the mailroom." He brushed a lock of dark hair out of his eyes and laughed at the memory. "The world's most boring job and back-breaking, and the pay is terrible. But it's the heart of the business and I've got to understand it."

The waiter was already back but Cynthia had barely begun to eat. She looked up at the overanxious waiter and drawled, "Nice chopped liver. Think the chef would like to trade recipes with my Aunt Helen?" The waiter gave her an outraged look and retreated.

"Why do I get the impression you aren't impressed?" Jim asked, watching her carefully. "You're pretty tough on the waiter."

"Stuck-up creep."

"Not really. He can tell you don't like him and he thinks he's lost his tip. These guys live on their tips."

She stared at him, amazed. He appeared not to notice.

"Think you'll pledge one of the sororities?" he asked, quickly changing the subject.

"Doubt if I'll have time." Or the money, or the clothes, or the background . . . "I have a heavy schedule. I didn't come here to goof around."

"You can't work all the time."

"I pretty much do."

"Then I'd better rescue you. You need some fun along with the work, and I'd love to be the one to give it to you." He smiled at her so warmly that her whole face lit up as she smiled back.

"Quite beautiful," he said quietly. "Soft everything—hair, eyes, even that extravagant sweater. I'm a lucky man and the waiter knows it." He paused in his compliment. "But seriously—won't you hypnotize me? Pretty please?"

They were on the way back to Hastings when Jim suddenly tugged at her arm.

"Hey, did you see that? Jungle Golf! I didn't know they had it up here."

"What's Jungle Golf?" She peered out the window, trying to follow his gaze. Jim made a U-turn and parked.

"You don't know Jungle Golf? It's fantastic. C'mon," he pleaded, half dragging her out of the van.

"What are you doing? You're crazy," she said a moment later as they found themselves standing in the freezing night air. "I don't even know where we are."

"Trust me." Jim threw an arm over her shoulders and ducked his head against the wind. "You're going to love it."

"Isn't this wonderful?" Jim asked happily fifteen minutes later. He lined up a trick shot into a lion's mouth. "We've got the whole place to ourselves."

"Surprise, surprise," Cynthia retorted. "Where can everyone be? Maybe—just maybe—they think it's closed for the season."

"You know, if you can shoot right through the giraffe's legs, there's a chance it'll bounce off the elephant's trunk and you get a hole in one. And that means you get a free game." He grinned at her, having the time of his life. "The last time I played, in South Carolina, I got four free games. Just think: we could be here all night!"

"Great. Then tomorrow they could set up our frozen remains as the new obstacle on the fourteenth hole." Cynthia leaned against a grotesque pink flamingo, feeling the biting wind whip around her legs. They were the only customers, and the teenage boy on duty had looked at them in amazement when Jim bought their tickets.

"You might want to take your time with that next shot," Jim said seriously. "It's a tough one. You'll have to stay a little to the right of the zebra or you'll end up in the lily

pond. But don't aim too high or you'll hit
the thatched hut." He picked up the ball
and headed for the next hole. She stayed
where she was, flapping her arms, trying to
warm up enough to hold the club. When
Jim realized that Cynthia wasn't following
him, he turned back in surprise. "Need
some help?" he asked. "It's really a snap if
you keep your eye on the ball and shoot
straight."

Cynthia hopped and flapped, imitating
the flamingo. "I think I can manage,
thanks." *To the right of the zebra, to the left
of the thatched hut . . .*

"Try to visualize where the ball's going,"
Jim called encouragingly.

"Do I talk when it's your shot?" It would
be fun to win, she thought suddenly. He
thinks he's the Arnold Palmer of Jungle
Golf. . . .

"And be sure you hit it hard enough to
clear the pond," Jim called from the side-
lines.

"Shut up," she yelled, giving the ball a
furious whack. It missed the zebra and by-
passed the hut, then hooked and caught a
metal hippopotamus in the stomach. The
noise was so funny and unexpected that
Cynthia burst out laughing and Jim joined
in.

"Where did the ball go?" She trudged
through the tangle of monkey grass.

"Here it is." Jim grinned triumphantly,
holding the ball in the air. "It bounced off

that palm tree and hit the hippo. Another few inches and you would have ruined him for life."

When they got back to Windsor Hall, Cynthia stopped on the front porch, turned to Jim, and said softly, "Thanks for everything. I had a great time."

Her hand was on the heavy brass doorknob, but Jim made no move to leave. Instead, he rested his hands lightly on her coat collar and smiled down at her.

"You're an ace at Jungle Golf, Cynthia. But next time, you pick the place."

"Next time?" She hadn't even thought about that.

"You didn't think I'd let you get away that easily, did you?"

"I'm not sure Jungle Golf is really my—"

But she didn't get a chance to finish. Jim bent down and kissed her very lightly on the lips.

"—game," she finished, a little breathlessly, when he released her. She was looking up into his eyes. "I wasn't expecting that," she said softly.

"Well, now that you are, let's do it right." Jim pulled her close. In a moment, Cynthia's arms were around his neck, her head snuggled close to his chin. "Next Saturday, right?" he murmured.

"Right."

Only a whole long week away . . .

Chapter 8

"Are we still speaking?" Agatha asked sleepily the next morning. She rolled over to look at the alarm clock and groaned. "And what in the world are you doing up so early?"

Cynthia buttoned the top button on her white uniform and grinned at her roommate. "Sure, we're still speaking, and I'm on my way to work." She pulled her hair back and pinned it with two tortoiseshell barrettes behind her ears. I wonder if Jim would like it better this way, she caught herself thinking.

Agatha sat up groggily and hugged her powder-blue electric blanket. "You're positively glowing this morning," she said shrewdly. "Something tells me my little white lie paid off."

"Little white lie?" Cynthia countered. "You told me a whopper."

"I figured it was the only way I could get you guys together. I guess I'm just a born matchmaker." She gave a giant yawn and regarded Cynthia with serious blue eyes. "But like they say, all's well that ends well. I gather the evening was a success."

"I suppose you could call it a success—all things considered." Cynthia smothered a laugh.

"That's all you're going to say? That it was *a success*?" Agatha was indignant. "Cynthia, you're unbelievable! You go out with one of the best catches on campus, and you make it sound like you yawned your way through the whole evening. What's wrong with you? Don't you get excited over anything? I had a pet rock that showed more enthusiasm than you do!" Agatha stopped to take a breath and Cynthia's laughter broke through Agatha's harangue.

"Okay, Agatha, I'll tell you the truth, even though I'm not sure you deserve it after that trick. Jim was terrific. I had such a great time I was tempted to wake you up last night to tell you all about it."

"Well, that's a little better," Agatha said, mollified. "For a moment I thought I had a zombie instead of a roommate. C'mon, don't keep me guessing. Where did you go and what did you do?"

"We went to The Landing for dinner and things got a lot better after that."

"Better? The Landing's one of the best restaurants in Boston." Agatha hopped out of bed. She winced when her feet hit the cold floor and grabbed for her robe.

"Yeah, but it's too fancy to relax in," Cynthia went on.

"Oh, is that so?" Agatha was hunting under the bed for her furry slippers. "Well, are you going out with him again?"

"Of course. Next Saturday. It's the most amazing thing, but I feel like I've known him forever. We laugh at the same kinds of crazy things, and . . . I don't know, we just never run out of things to say."

"Sounds serious," Agatha said lightly.

"Oh, nothing like that." Cynthia flushed. "I don't want to rush it." She gave a little laugh, wondering if it was true.

"Don't you? Well, I do. When you run across the real thing . . . you just know. I knew Bud was right for me the moment I met him. I just looked in his eyes and that was it."

"Well, it was different with Jim and me," Cynthia said. She thought a moment. "But maybe not *much* different."

Later that morning, when Cynthia was dishing out pancakes in the cafeteria, she caught herself daydreaming about Jim Terkel. Judging from the amused looks she got from her co-workers, she was sure that she was wearing a permanent grin on her face. She couldn't stop smiling, even when Adelle Maris jumped the line looking for orange juice.

"I'm afraid we're out of orange," Cynthia said pleasantly. "Why don't you try prune?

It might be just what you need." Her expression was innocent. For a moment the two girls stared at each other, and then Adelle grabbed a glass of grapefruit juice and stalked away, leaving Jacqui Orsini in a fit of giggles.

"That's called living dangerously," she said to Cynthia. "Did you see the look on her face when you said prune juice? She's probably planning some diabolical revenge right this minute."

"I didn't like the way she barged in ahead of you," Cynthia said, smiling at the pretty redhead. "And speaking of living dangerously, I hear you're a terror at the wheel." She'd been surprised by the rumor that Jacqui was taking up race-car driving—it was the last thing in the world she'd expect from a girl who wanted to be a concert violinist.

"Terror at the wheel?" Jacqui said, puzzled. She helped herself to a sweet roll. "Oh, you must have heard about my friend from Cornell Hall. I met a guy there who has this real hot Trans Am," she explained, "and he lets me drive it."

"She doesn't drive it, she flies it," Margot Williams piped up. "Next, she'll be trying out for the Indy 500."

"Hey, wouldn't that be fantastic!" Jacqui said, beaming. "But I've got a long way to go before that." She smiled, sliding her tray farther down the line.

"How's the coffee cake, Cynthia?"

Margot Williams asked, studying a tray of pastries. "Or haven't you had a chance to try it?"

"I'm on a diet," Cynthia said. "I think I ate five pounds of shrimp at The Landing last night."

"The Landing?" Margot grinned appreciatively. "Your date's got class. Who is he?"

"Jim Terkel," Cynthia said with a little glow of pride. "I met him at the Phi Delt house." She turned to the next person in line, feeling a rush of warmth in her cheeks. *Jim Terkel.* She could hardly believe her good luck.

"She's certainly happy," Margot said a few minutes later as she slid into a seat next to Adelle.

"Who?" Adelle Maris asked in a bored voice.

"Cynthia Woyzek," Margot said, glancing over at the serving line. "It must be that guy Jim Terkel she went out with last night. It sounds like he's the new love in her life."

"Jim Terkel?" Adelle mused. "Well, now it finally makes sense. She's looking for a meal ticket."

"What do you mean?" Jacqui demanded. "He's probably a really nice guy."

"He's also a really rich guy," Adelle said pointedly. "As far as Cynthia's concerned, money talks. She wouldn't care if he had two heads, as long as he's loaded."

"Come on, Adelle, have a heart. Cynthia's poor but proud," Margot objected.

Adelle laughed bitterly. "The hell she is. She told me the first day she was here that she was out to marry money. What do you think she came to college for—to learn to sling hash? She can do that back in Detroit."

"She really said that?" Jacqui said wonderingly.

"Why would I make it up? She probably made sure Mr. Phi Delt took her to an expensive place too. People like her always grab whatever they can get."

"They went to The Landing for dinner," Margot offered.

"What did I tell you? She picked the most expensive restaurant in Boston—I knew it. She probably took the leftovers home in a doggy bag."

There was a long, uncomfortable silence. Finally Jacqui cleared her throat and invited everyone to watch her compete in a NASCAR race the following week.

When Cynthia first spotted Sandi at a corner table in Harry's that evening, she did a double take. What's happened to her? she thought, shocked. Her sister had aged ten years. She was pale and haggard and her once-lustrous brown hair hung limp to her shoulders. Her face lit up when she saw

Cynthia, though, and the old brightness in her eyes shone.

"Honey, how are you? It's wonderful to see you."

"I'm doing great. How are you?" Cynthia took a seat across the table from Sandi. Even the muted light from a hurricane lamp couldn't disguise the heavy dark shadows under Sandi's eyes. "You look like you've lost some weight. Not on one of those crash diets again, are you?"

"Are you kidding? I still haven't recovered from that yogurt-and-wheat-germ kick we tried last summer. Remember? We'd starve ourselves all week—"

"And then eat pizza all weekend." Cynthia laughed. "It's the only time I ever managed to gain five pounds while dieting."

They were silent for a moment as Sandi began idly shredding her paper napkin into little pieces. "I know you're wondering why I'm here," she began nervously, keeping her eyes fixed firmly on the small pile of paper in front of her.

"I figured you just couldn't stand to be apart from your kid sister," Cynthia said, trying for a light tone.

"As modest as ever, I see." Sandi smiled wryly. There was a long pause and Cynthia wondered if she was ever going to get to the point. "The truth is . . . I've had a lot of problems at home—with Neil, I mean. I needed to get away for a while." She finally looked up, and there was a bruised look in her eyes that Cynthia hadn't noticed before.

"You mean like a vacation? You're going to stay here for a couple of days?"

"I'm going to be here for a long time, Cynthia," Sandi said quietly. "Maybe for good."

"What do you mean? Are you and Neil going to move to Boston?"

"Not Neil, just me. Neil and I . . . well, we've had our problems."

"Is it—is it somebody else?" For some reason Cynthia felt shy about asking her sister.

"No, I wish it were that simple," Sandi said with a bitter laugh. "Another woman is something I can handle."

"Then what?" Cynthia was shocked to see that Sandi's eyes were filling with tears.

"He . . . uh . . . hits me," Sandi said, biting her lip. "A lot." She turned her face to the side and Cynthia could see a faint bruise mark along her jawline. "Most of it's faded by now," Sandi went on dully, "but the last time he busted two of my teeth. It'll take me a month's salary to get them fixed."

"My God!" Cynthia was shocked. She thought of the last time she'd seen Neil. It had been at a Fourth of July cookout, and he'd had too much to drink.

"Nobody knows except you, so don't say anything, okay?"

"Nobody knows? What's wrong with you? The creep should be in jail."

"What good would that do? I'll need him

to help support me if he ever gets work. And he sure can't while he's in jail."

"Sandi, that's not the point. You can't just let someone beat you up and not do anything." She saw from her sister's expression that it was futile to argue with her. Cynthia tried another tack. "You're going to leave him, right? At least tell me that you're going to divorce him."

"I think so," Sandi said nervously, licking her lips. "But it's not as simple as you think. I've got to hire a lawyer, and he might fight it. There's about a million things to think about. That's why I came here." She reached across the table to grasp Cynthia's hand. "I had to get away, to have some time by myself to try to figure out what to do with my life."

"What are you going to do here?"

"Well, I've got a little room on the edge of town. It's nothing fancy, but it's right on the bus line."

"Bus line?"

Sandi nodded. "On Monday I'm going to start looking for a job. That's one good thing about being a beautician. You can always find work, anyplace in the world. No matter where you go, women are always going to want to get their hair done." She laughed mirthlessly. "So I've really got it made, haven't I? Five years of marriage and I end up in a strange town with no money, looking for a job."

Cynthia sipped her beer and remembered

the day she came home from school to learn that her older sister was getting married.

"How could you do this to us, Sandi?" Her father had been standing in the kitchen, shouting, and her mother was crying softly. Cynthia remembered how her father broke off when he saw her staring at them and said in a defeated tone, "You tell her, Sandi. Let's hear you try to explain it."

"I'm marrying Neil. Right away."

"Don't you want to go to college?" Cynthia had blurted out.

"I don't have a choice. I'm pregnant." And Sandi bolted from the room.

The wedding took place the following Saturday. The pregnancy ended in a miscarriage a few weeks later, but Sandi's marriage to Neil had continued until now.

Sandi's voice cut into her thoughts. "Hey honey, don't look like that. It's not the end of the world. I'll figure something out." She stood up and reached for the bill. "I wish I could do something to make you feel better."

"You can," Sandi said brightly. "How about giving me a grand tour of the campus next week? Who knows—maybe I'll be a college girl myself someday. You know, you didn't get all the brains in the family, little sister."

Chapter 9

"So this is what a college dorm is like. It's a lot different than I expected." Sandi's eyes flickered over the grass-green bedspreads and matching chintz drapes. "It looks like a Holiday Inn. I figured there'd be panty hose hanging all over the place and a dozen girls sharing a bathroom."

"The part about the bathroom is true. You should see what it's like on a Saturday night when everybody's getting ready to go out at the same time."

"You haven't said much about this guy of yours. I guess he's pretty special, isn't he?"

"Very special," Cynthia said softly.

"Well, make sure you play the field, honey. You've got plenty of time to look around and see what's out there. By the way, how are the girls in the dorm treating you? Your roommate looked like she's rolling in dough. Is she one of those society types?"

"Oh no, Agatha's nothing like that. She's got money, but she's no snob." Cynthia glanced out the window. The sky was overcast and the campus looked gloomy. "I almost fainted when I saw her clothes, though. She wears designer panty hose every day—those tinted ones at six bucks a shot."

"I saw the way she was dolled up this morning," Sandi said dryly, perching on the edge of the bed. "Wasn't that a mink-lined raincoat?"

"From Neiman's." Cynthia giggled. "She wears it to the library."

"You're kidding!" Sandi howled. "What does she wear on dates? Oscar de la Renta dresses?"

"Actually, she prefers Adolfo." Cynthia tried to keep a straight face. "She says that he's the only designer who really understands color—"

She was interrupted by a light tap on the door. "Agatha, can I borrow that light blue scarf—" It was Adelle Maris. She did a double take when she saw Sandi. "Oh, I'm sorry, Cynthia. I didn't know you had company." She flashed a toothy smile at Sandi and waited to be introduced.

"Agatha's at the library," Cynthia said curtly, "and this isn't company. This is my sister Sandi."

"Sandi! How nice to meet you," Adelle gushed, crossing the room to shake hands.

She turned to Cynthia. "I didn't know your sister went to Hastings."

"I don't," Sandi said easily. "I'm just visiting. I work in Boston."

Cynthia steeled herself for what was coming. "Oh really? What do you do?" Adelle's smile widened.

"I'm a hairstylist."

"A beautician! How interesting." Her shrewd eyes roamed over Sandi's polyester pants and thin sweater. "That must be really nice for you, Cynthia. I bet Sandi gives you all sorts of beauty tips."

"Cynthia doesn't need any help," Sandi said with a faint smile. "She's terrific just the way she is."

"Oh, of course she is," Adelle purred. "You're absolutely right. Tell Agatha I stopped by, will you sweetie? It was really nice to meet you, Sandi." She swept out the door.

"What a charmer," Sandi said as soon as Adelle was out of earshot. "I thought you said the girls here were okay."

"Adelle's the exception that proves the rule. I don't know what the problem is, but she took a dislike to me the day we met. We've been at each other's throat ever since."

"A personality clash," Sandi said, nodding. "It happens. Well, don't let it bother you, little sister. From what I can see, Adelle isn't anyone you want to hang out with anyway."

* * *

"I just met Cynthia Woyzek's sister," Adelle told Susan a few minutes later. "God, what a loser." She gave a world-weary sigh and collapsed into a desk chair.

"Is she that bad?" Susan marked the place in her French book and set it aside.

"She's just like Cynthia, total loss. A beautician! Can you believe it?"

"Cynthia's not as bad as you think," Susan said mildly, rubbing her fingers together. "Besides, somebody has to cut hair. Just be glad it isn't you. Work isn't your style." She gave Adelle a sly look. "Betty Berke tells me Cynthia and Jim Terkel are a hot item."

Adelle ground her teeth. "Little Miss Carrot-top herself. I've noticed the two of them are always together." Adelle thought for a minute, then smiled. She'd come to a decision at last. She was going to bring Cynthia down in flames. And Betty Berke was going to help her.

Unlocking the blue leather diary she kept in her bottom drawer, Betty curled up on the window seat, looking over her last entry. *Dear Mitch*, she'd written in violet ink, *I'm writing to you in my diary because I'll probably never get a chance to say these things to you in person. I wish there were some way you could know what's in my heart. My darling Mitch, I haven't been able to get you out of my mind since we met at*

*the Phi Delt party so many weeks ago. I
think of you at odd times of the day—when
I'm studying, walking to class, talking to my
friends. In fact, I probably think of you
every hour on the hour! I'm hooked on you,
hopelessly, totally, with all my heart and
soul. I can only hope that someday this
magic love I feel will rub off on you, and
that we can spend our lives together.*

A sharp knock on the door made Betty
jump, and she tucked the diary under a
Bride magazine.

"Hi, Betty." It was Adelle. "Did I catch
you at a bad time?"

"No, I'm just doing some studying," Betty
mumbled, her cheeks burning.

"Oh, I see." Adelle glanced at the desk.
There wasn't a textbook in sight. "I just
dropped by to say hi. It's been awhile since
we've had a chance to chat, so I thought I'd
make sure you were okay." She smiled
warmly.

"That's really nice of you." Betty was
flattered. She had never thought that Adelle
liked her. It just went to show how wrong
you could be about people.

"Did you do anything exciting Saturday
night?" Adelle inquired. "I figured all the
fraternity boys would be giving you a big
rush. Red hair always turns guys on."

"No," Betty said regretfully. "I stayed in
all weekend. I met a guy a few weeks ago,
but I'm still waiting for him to call."

"Well, I'm sure he will." Adelle gave her a

warm smile. "You've really got to watch out for those fraternity guys, though."

"What do you mean?"

"Well, you know the way guys like to talk, and the Greeks are the worst. You should have heard what one of them was saying about Cynthia Woyzek." She laughed. "Of course, there's not a grain of truth in it, but stories like that can really hurt a girl's reputation."

"You mean some guy was talking about Cynthia? What did he say?"

"Everyone's saying it by now." Adelle took a seat on Daphne's bed. "His name was Jim something . . . Terkel, that was it. Anyway, I heard he said that Cynthia only had two words in her vocabulary—yeah and sure. Isn't that a scream? She'll do it with anybody, can you imagine? He's just going to string her along till he gets what he wants and . . . well, you get the picture."

"That's terrible," Betty said weakly. "How could he say a thing like that?"

"Oh well, guys will be guys." Adelle shrugged. "Did I tell you what happened to me in English class the other day? We have a new professor and—"

But Betty wasn't listening. How could Jim Terkel be such a bastard! she wondered to herself. And Cynthia *adored* him!

A few minutes later, Adelle left for the library. Betty threw on her coat and muffler and headed out for a long walk around the lake. She needed time to think, to decide what to do about Cynthia. How do you tell your best friend that her boyfriend is a rat?

The next couple of days flew by for Cynthia. Before she knew it, Thursday night had rolled around. She was studying in her room when there was a light knock on the door.

"C'mon in," she called, glad to have a chance to close her textbook. The question of the unification of Germany had long ago ceased to fascinate her.

"You're studying," Betty Berke observed. "Maybe I should come back later."

"Hey, don't be silly." Cynthia looked at her friend questioningly. Betty seemed strangely ill at ease. "What's up?"

"Oh, no problem, I just wanted to see how you were doing." Betty attempted a smile that froze on her lips. She sank into the battered easy chair.

Cynthia studied her for a moment. Outwardly she looked the same. The same tousled mop of red hair, the suspender pants with the striped T-shirt that made her look like a character in *Godspell* . . . but something was wrong. Her infectious grin was absent. Betty's eyes had a veiled, troubled look that Cynthia hadn't seen before.

"Cynthia, I have to tell you something." Betty's tone was anguished.

"What's wrong?" Cynthia stared at her friend. "I knew you had something on your mind from the moment you walked in here."

"You're right," Betty said in a little voice. "I wish there was some easy way to tell you, but there isn't, so . . ."

"Oh, come on. It can't be as bad as all that."

"It is." Betty swallowed hard. "I'm afraid it's worse than you can imagine. It's about you—and Jim Terkel."

"About me and Jim?" There was a catch in Cynthia's voice. "But I've only gone out with him once." She had already told Betty everything about the fantastic "blind" date. "Hey, if it's something about him and other girls, I don't want to hear it." Her voice held more assurance than she felt.

"No, that's not it," Betty said miserably. "He's been spreading stories about you."

"What do you mean?" Cynthia's heart was hammering furiously. "What kind of stories?"

"He's told all the guys in Phi Delt how easy you are. He said you'll make it with anyone. He was only taking you out for kicks. As soon as he . . . uh . . . gets what he wants from you, he's going to drop you. Cynthia, he's actually bragging about it."

"Who told you that? I don't believe he said any such thing." Cynthia turned her face from her friend. All of a sudden, her wonderful evening with Jim Terkel seemed like a joke, a cruel hoax.

"I didn't want to tell you," Betty said plaintively, "but it's all over school. I stayed awake half the night wondering what to do." She stood up uncertainly. "Then I finally decided that if it was me . . . well, I'd rather know the truth no matter how much it hurt."

"Slow down, Betty. It's not such a big deal," Cynthia tried to make her voice sound casual. "We had a good time together, but it's not like the love affair of the century or anything. If Jim's into playing games—" Her voice broke suddenly, then she caught herself. "Who needs him, right?" She took a deep breath before she turned around. "I'm glad you told me, Betty. You did the right thing."

"Then why do I feel so awful?" Betty wailed. "You looked so happy when I came in."

"I'm still happy." Cynthia tried to smile. "Believe me, Jim Terkel isn't worth losing any sleep over." Cynthia grabbed her coat. "Hey, I've got to get to the library before it closes. If I don't do better for Aldridge, it's pink-slip time for sure."

"Are you sure you feel okay?" Betty's brow was furrowed.

"Of course I'm okay. Why wouldn't I be?" Cynthia picked up her notebook. "Let's get a pizza tomorrow night, okay? I'll pay. Look, I've really got to run. The rise of the middle class awaits!" She grinned and dashed out the door.

Cynthia didn't stop until she had reached the first-floor landing. Then she leaned against the wall, forcing herself to take deep breaths. She felt sick. How could Jim do this to her? He'd seemed so wonderful, so caring and she'd fallen like a stone.

Cynthia heard voices. Quickly, she tried to pull herself together. By the time Adelle Maris and Susan McMahon rounded the corner, she was cool and composed.

"Hello, Cynthia," they chorused. They exchanged arch smiles, and Cynthia wondered if they suspected she'd been crying.

Let them think what they want, she decided wearily. She nodded briefly and moved on, dreading the cold walk to the library. She felt numb, but she knew that sometime before Saturday night she'd have to force herself to think. She still had to decide what to do about Jim Terkel.

"I wonder what's wrong with her?" Susan whispered as she and Adelle made their way up the stairs. "She's as white as a sheet."

"Maybe she heard some bad news," Adelle said lightly.

"Bad? From the look on her face, I'd say it was catastrophic."

A slow smile spread over Adelle's face.

She turned to her friend. "Well, I certainly hope so," she purred.

Susan's eyes widened in surprise. "Adelle, you're really awful. Poor Cynthia doesn't deserve that!"

"Oh yes, she does," her friend said calmly.

Chapter 10

"So you decided to go anyway." Betty Berke was sitting cross-legged on Cynthia's bed, watching as Cynthia dressed for her date with Jim Terkel.

"I may be making the biggest mistake of my life," Cynthia said grimly. "I nearly called him half a dozen times to cancel out."

"Oh, I'm glad you didn't. He deserves another chance. After all, maybe the whole thing is just a giant misunderstanding. Maybe he's just as terrific as we thought he was in the beginning."

"You're such an optimist." Cynthia smiled at her friend. "You alway give everybody the benefit of the doubt."

"Well, of course I do. It would be crazy to break up with someone like Jim Terkel and then find out you were wrong about him. I've got a feeling the two of you really belong together."

"Don't get your hopes up." Cynthia turned from the mirror with a determined look on her face. "My sister made a fool of herself over a man, and I don't plan on doing the same thing. If Jim Terkel's a bastard, I'm going to find it out one way or the other—and I'm going to find it out tonight."

"You're pretty quiet tonight," Jim said. "Maybe we should have gone to the mixer instead of the movie." It was nearly eleven, and they were sipping hot chocolate at the Student Center before heading back to Windsor Hall.

"No, the movie was fine," Cynthia said tightly. The last thing in the world she wanted was to have Jim's arms wrapped around her while they slow-danced.

"I have to confess, this is the third time I've seen *10*." Jim laughed.

"You must like it," Cynthia said shortly.

"Who wouldn't like Bo Derek?"

"Judging from the audience response, the male population at Hastings agrees with you." Cynthia took a gulp of hot chocolate and nearly scalded herself.

"Yeah, they got a little carried away, didn't they?" Jim laughed tolerantly. "Well, guys are like that, Cynthia."

"What? Loud and obnoxious?"

He looked puzzled. "What's bugging you tonight?" He put his arm around her and nuzzled her cheek, but she ducked away.

"Nothing's wrong," she said coolly. "I guess the movie just reminded me how stupid and superficial most of the guys around here are. They thought it was great that Dudley Moore dumped Julie Andrews just so he could go after some strange chick who turned him on. That's supposed to be comedy?"

"Cynthia, it's just a movie," Jim protested. When she didn't answer, he leaned forward and cupped his hand under her chin. "I sure would like to know what's bothering you tonight. You're not like yourself at all."

"No? Well, maybe you don't know what I'm really like. Maybe you don't know anything about me." Every time she thought of the rumors, Cynthia felt a dull ache inside. She never should have accepted another date with Jim—it hurt too much to be near him.

"I know a lot about you," he said softly. "I know that you're a wonderful girl . . . and very soft under this Eskimo getup." He laughed, pinching her heavy winter coat.

"And that's all you need to know, right?" She pushed his hand away.

"Oh no," he said playfully, "there are a lot of other things I'd like to find out, but unfortunately, this isn't the time or place." He sighed and glanced around the crowded coffee shop. "Now, if we were back at the Phi Delt house, in my room—"

"Is that where you take your one-night stands?"

"Oh, you'd definitely be a two-night

stand," he said. "Probably even a week-ender."

Cynthia jumped up so quickly she over-turned her hot chocolate. It sloshed all over the table.

"Sorry, Terkel, I don't happen to be a weekender," she said furiously. "Especially not yours." Cynthia charged out of the coffee shop. After an instant of shocked surprise, Jim threw some money on the table and scrambled after her.

"Hey, what's wrong with you?" he de-manded when he caught up with her out-side. "It was a joke, for crying out loud."

"Maybe I'm sick of being taken in by guys," she choked. "Especially fraternity types with their alligator sweaters and their lousy jokes." Tears welled up in her eyes. Cynthia angrily brushed them away.

"Look, if I came on too strong, I'm sorry."

"Just forget it," she snapped. "I was wrong to go out with you in the beginning. Next time I'll trust my instincts."

"What do you mean, instincts? Cynthia, you know I want to see you again . . ."

"Never in a million years!"

"Cynthia, it was a joke—all right? I mean, it wasn't a joke, I really like you, I'm crazy about you—wait, this is all nuts!"

But Cynthia was already tearing across the main quad. Jim had to dash after her. When he caught up, she stopped dead in her tracks and glared at him. Tears stung her eyes. "You think this is *nuts*? Is that what you think? You've got a hell of a nerve, Terkel. You really do. Well, if this is so nuts, why don't you just forget me—okay? Because it would be a *big favor.*"

Jim put out an arm to stop her, but Cynthia angrily brushed it aside and hurried down the path. He stared after her until she was out of sight, then sighed and shook his head.

"Women," he muttered.

Cynthia took the steps to Windsor Hall two at a time, determined not to break down until she was safely inside her room. With any luck Agatha would be talking to Bud and Cynthia would have time to pull herself together. Why had she subjected herself to this evening? It had been a terrible mistake to see him again.

She tore open the door to the common room to find Agatha sprawled in the easy chair. "Home early?" Agatha inquired cheerfully. "I thought dates with Jim Terkel could go on forever."

"Don't mention that creep's name to me ever again." Cynthia yanked off her coat and threw herself into the opposite chair.

"What happened?"

"Jim and I broke up. Not that we had anything going anyway." She eyed her short-trimmed fingernails, afraid that if she looked up, she'd burst into tears.

"I'm really sorry." Agatha sounded surprised. "If you want to talk about it—"

"There's nothing to talk about."

"I don't understand," Agatha protested. "You two had such a great time together. Did something happen—"

"Look, I just don't want to discuss it, okay? Please!" Seeing Agatha's hurt expression, Cynthia added, "I was wrong about him. Let's just leave it at that."

"All right," Agatha said after a long pause. "I won't mention it again. But it doesn't make sense to me."

Cynthia did not reply.

After a few minutes Agatha got up quietly and went into the bedroom.

When the door had closed, Cynthia shut her book and allowed herself a small, bitter laugh. "You know something?" she said barely above a whisper. "It doesn't make sense to me either."

Chapter 11

During the next few days, Cynthia felt like her whole life was thrown into fast forward. She rushed from classes to the cafeteria to the library, eating on the run, squeezing in her assignments at spare moments, rarely getting to bed before midnight. She did her best to block all thoughts of Jim Terkel from her mind, but she still worried about Sandi.

Every time she considered her sister's options, she came up against a brick wall. Sandi should divorce Neil—that was obvious—but she also needed a new career, new training, perhaps even the chance to go to college. But all that took money, which neither of them had.

When she met Sandi for dinner on Friday night, her sister was shocked at her appearance. "Honestly, Cynthia, you don't look well. You're doing too much."

"Don't be silly," Cynthia answered tiredly. "A little hard work never killed anyone."

"Tell me about it. Remember how Dad used to say I was lazy? If he could see me now, he'd eat his words."

There was an embarrassed pause and Cynthia said hesitantly, "I guess you haven't told them anything about you and Neil."

"No, of course I haven't," Sandi bit into a corned-beef sandwich. "And don't you dare tell them, either. The last thing I need is for them to get in on the act. They never were too crazy about Neil, if you remember."

"They'll have to know eventually. You're going to divorce him, aren't you?"

"I guess so. Look, do we have to talk about it now? This is the first treat I've had in a week." Sandi looked around the Sub Station, a popular sandwich bar in South Boston. "I was hoping we could relax for a couple of hours and not talk about anything unpleasant." She took a long swig from her frosted mug and said gratefully, "I've been dying for a beer all day."

"Sandi," Cynthia began, "I don't want to sound like Mom, but one of us has got to face facts."

"What facts?" Sandi asked warily. She motioned to the waitress to refill her own beer mug and Cynthia's root beer.

"Well, the fact that you're going to need money, for one thing. You said you're not getting any from Neil, so how are you managing?"

"I get by. The pay isn't great at the beauty

shop, but like they say, it's a living. And rent is cheap over on South Street. Not that I want to stay there forever."

"I should hope not," Cynthia said fervently. They'd stopped in Sandi's room briefly before dinner, and the memory of the dingy hallway with its pungent smell of boiled cabbage was still with her. "The place is a fleabag and a firetrap."

Sandi smiled. "Anyway, I may be moving soon. Just as soon as I get some money together."

"How are you going to do that? I thought you said the tips were lousy."

"They are." Sandi took a long swig of her beer and grinned. "But didn't I tell you? I'm going to moonlight at a couple of the big hotels. In fact, I've got my first job at the Carillon tomorrow night at six."

"You're working at a hotel?"

"Yeah. Terry, one of the girls I work with, told me about it. A lot of hotel beauty shops close at five, so they use free-lancers like me in the evening. From what I've heard, those hotel customers really lay on the tips. It's always a case of, 'Quick, make me presentable, I'm having dinner with the sheik of Arabia.' You can clear forty or fifty dollars in the early evening." She smiled happily. "I go to the room and usually they've already washed their hair in the shower. I just do a blow-dry and maybe a hot-curl. Takes twenty minutes, tops. I carry everything with me."

"It sounds like a great idea," Cynthia said. They were silent for a moment while the waitress put a beer and a root beer in front of them. "I hope you're going to reconsider and tell Mom and Dad about Neil, though. You can't hide out forever."

"I know," Sandi said, a shadow crossing her face. "I told them I came for a styling convention, but they're not going to buy that much longer."

"So when are you going to tell them the truth?"

"I don't know." Sandi reached across the table to pat Cynthia's hand. "You know something, little sister? You worry too much."

"Somebody has to."

The talk turned to family members and Sandi told a long, funny story about a Labor Day picnic that Cynthia had missed. Cynthia laughed at Sandi's imitation of a grandaunt, but the story made her feel a little homesick. Later, when they parted company outside the restaurant, Cynthia glanced at her watch and got another surprise.

She'd been so caught up in Sandi's problems that she had managed to go a whole two hours without thinking of Jim Terkel.

"This is not the ideal way to spend a Saturday night," Betty Berke moaned to Cynthia. The two girls were sitting on

Betty's bed, flipping through fashion magazines. "Do you want to go to Kennett Square and see a movie?"

"I'm waiting for a phone call from my sister."

"Oh yeah." Betty tossed aside a *Vogue* and reached for a *Cosmo*. "You told me about her. Maybe she'd like to come with us."

"I don't think so. She's been working seven days a week, and she's really wiped out."

"Well, she can't work all the time, can she?" Betty ran a hand through her tangled red curls and made a face. "You must come from a family of workaholics."

Cynthia smiled and reached for another magazine. "You're the first person I've ever met who subscribes to *Modern Bride*."

"Really?" Betty remarked. "I've saved every copy for the past four years."

"You're kidding," Cynthia hooted.

"Well, they've got a lot of good information in them," Betty said defensively. "You find out what the latest styles are in wedding dresses"—she flushed when Cynthia snickered—"and how to pick out china and silver. Anytime you want to borrow some, just help yourself."

"China and silver? I think you're barking up the wrong tree. We come from different worlds, Betty. When my sister got married, she furnished her whole apartment in Early Goodwill." She laughed and tossed the magazine aside. "Anyway, don't you think it's a little premature, planning your wedding? In case you haven't noticed, we don't even have dates for tonight."

"I know," Betty's smile faded. "I had hoped Mitch would call, but I guess it's not in the cards." She hesitated. "You never told me what happened on your last date with Jim."

"I've tried to block it out of my mind," Cynthia said, swallowing hard. "I was trying to figure out a way to ask him about the rumors when he . . . uh . . . made some joke about me being a one-night stand. Just what I needed to hear, right?"

"That's awful," Betty said softly. "I still feel rotten about being the one to tell you."

"Hey, don't be silly. I would have found out anyway, you know. At least you broke it to me gently." She stood and headed for the door. "Catch you tomorrow, okay? Sandi will be calling any minute."

She left Betty happily engrossed in a four-page spread on winter weddings. Just as Cynthia turned the corridor corner, the phone rang.

It was Sandi.

"Cynthia, you should be over at the Carillon tonight," her sister said excitedly. "I've already made twenty-five dollars in tips, and guess what? There's a bunch of kids from Hastings here."

"From Hastings? What's going on?"

"I think it's a sorority dance. They've taken over the main ballroom and hired three bands. These kids must have a lot of dough."

"How late are you going to work?" Cynthia asked, suddenly restless. "Maybe we could catch a late movie—"

"Oh honey, I'd love to, but I'm really swamped. I've got four more heads to do. One client even wants her hair braided." She paused. "Aren't you going out on a date tonight? I thought you said you were seeing someone."

"I was, but it didn't work out." The last thing Cynthia wanted to do was get into a discussion about Jim Terkel. "Plenty more where that one came from."

"Ah, you're seeing the light!" Suddenly the sugary strains of "Chances Are" drifted over the wires. "Someone just opened the door to the ballroom. I can't hear a thing. Talk to you tomorrow, okay? And don't study too hard, sis."

"No, I won't."

Cynthia hung up.

Betty Berke watched enviously as her roommate, Daphne Riesling, drenched herself with Arpege.

"I thought you were just supposed to put perfume on your pulse points. You're practically taking a bath in it."

"I don't want to leave anything to chance. Who knows where Chuck will strike next?"

Daphne grinned and sprinkled a few drops down her bra. "I hope to hell he doesn't stop with my pulse points. That's just the beginning. Uh-oh," she said, noting Betty's red face. "I hate to tell you, but you're doing it again, kid."

"Ohmigosh." Betty's hands flew to her crimson cheeks. "I thought living with you had cured me of that."

Daphne shook her head in disbelief. "You've got to be the only girl in Windsor Hall who still blushes. Probably the only girl at Hastings." She slipped into a white rabbit coat.

"I know, I hate it. It makes me feel like I'm twelve years old."

"Don't knock it, roomy. I think it's kind of cute. A lot of guys go for the sweet, old-fashioned type." She flipped her thick blond hair over the collar of the coat and studied the effect in the mirror. "What do you think of my new lip gloss?" She made a sexy pout. "Is it too orangey?"

"No, you look perfect, just perfect." She watched Daphne toss an apricot wool muffler over her shoulders and grab her crushed leather purse.

"Chuck may borrow a friend's apartment, so don't call out the goon squad if I don't show up tonight. And for God's sake, find something to do besides study," Daphne ordered on her way out the door.

"Is that who I think it is?" Adelle Maris

said softly to Claire Rhodes, the junior who had sponsored her at the Sigma Chi dance.

"Who?" Claire looked around the crowded lobby of the Carillon.

"Nothing," Adelle answered. "I thought I recognized someone, that's all. It must be someone else."

"We better get back to our dates." Claire started across the lobby.

"I'll catch up with you, okay? I want to buy some cigarettes." Adelle turned swiftly toward the reception desk. She was positive she had seen Cynthia Woyzek's sister standing there, deep in conversation with the bellhop. Sandi—that was her name. She'd met her the other day when Cynthia brought her to the dorm. A real nobody, just the person you'd expect to be the sister of the hash slinger from Detroit.

And here she was, in the lobby of the Carillon Hotel, talking to the bellhop. Talking business, maybe? Adelle edged closer, taking in Sandi's shabby coat and overnight bag.

My God, she must be a hooker, Adelle thought delightedly. Little Cynthia Woyzek's sister is an honest-to-God hooker. She snickered at the thought.

"You're lined up for 305, 612, and 437 tonight," the bellhop was saying. He watched while Sandi carefully wrote down the room numbers on a pad. "There should be good money there," he added.

"I hope so. I can sure use it," Sandi said feelingly, flashing him a smile.

Adelle watched her cross the lobby. Cynthia Woyzek's sister, a hooker! She still couldn't believe her luck. If she hadn't agreed to go to this silly sorority dance, she never would have discovered the truth.

" 'And the truth shall make you free,' " she muttered under her breath. By Monday morning, half of Hastings would know the whole truth about Cynthia's sister.

Chapter 12

"I don't believe it," Margot Williams declared. "Not Cynthia's sister." It was Sunday afternoon and Adelle had invited a few girls to share a bottle of wine with her in her room. She had waited patiently for Jacqui Orsini and Daphne Riesling to arrive before she dropped the bomb.

"So what, even if she is a hooker?" Daphne poured herself a hefty serving of Chablis. "Live and let live, I say."

"Maybe it was somebody who looked like Sandi," Margot insisted. Her dark eyes were troubled, and she ran her hand nervously through her gleaming Afro. "After all, you said the lobby at the Carillon was crowded last night."

"Not that crowded." Adelle smirked. "And I made sure I got a really close look at her. She was standing at the desk. I could even hear the bellboy tell her what room numbers to go to."

"Well, if she's a hooker, she picked a good place to work," Daphne said cheerfully.

"There are four big conventions booked in Boston next week."

Jacqui Orsini scowled. "Hey, you guys are jumping to an awful lot of conclusions awfully fast."

Adelle stood up quickly and opened another bottle of wine. "If that's what you call putting two and two together—fine, I'm coming to a lot of conclusions." She popped the cork, poured herself a glass, and passed the bottle. "How about Cynthia? Anyone know how she picks up spending money?"

Jacqui was openmouthed. "Adelle, I don't believe you."

"Just asking, you know." Adelle shrugged.

"Well, I doubt it." The opinion was offered by Daphne, who was stretched out on the floor. Tucking a throw pillow behind her head, she stared thoughtfully at the ceiling. "You should hear the way Betty talks about Cynthia. You'd think she was a saint."

"Yeah, and that's *Betty* for you," Adelle pointed out. "Betty thinks anyone who doesn't smoke, drink, or snort is a saint. So Cynthia plays the professional virgin in front of her."

"You think it's an act?" Nan Deluca was lighting up a joint. "I don't know Cynthia very well, but I always figured she was pretty upfront. I mean, all the Detroit stuff —she admits it. She doesn't try to pretend she's from Miss Porter's or anything."

"Well, she might be honest about her background," Adelle observed. "But she makes no secret about liking money. She told me she came here for one reason—to catch a rich guy. The more power to her, if that's what she wants." Adelle smiled.

"Got a minute, Betty?" Agatha Mitchell caught up with Betty Berke on the steps of the library.

"Sure. In fact, I've got three and a half hours." Betty made a face. "That's how much time I've allowed myself to work on my history paper."

"When's it due?" Agatha shifted her books to one arm and pushed open the heavy glass door.

"Approximately tomorrow." Betty fluffed her curly red hair and sighed. "I'm a terrible procrastinator."

They settled themselves at one of the heavy oak tables in the reading room. Agatha leaned forward. "This morning, I found out something about Cynthia Woyzek."

"Really? What is it?"

"She's got a birthday coming up next week. Cynthia would never say a word about it, but I happened to see a card from her sister. Do you want to help me organize a surprise party for her? We'll get all the girls in the dorm together and chip in for cake and wine—"

"That's a fantastic idea!" Betty interrupted her. "She could use some cheering up."

"So you noticed too," Agatha said thoughtfully. "What do you think it's about?"

"I've . . . uh . . . got no idea," Betty stammered. Why, she wondered, had she opened her big mouth? If Cynthia had wanted Agatha to know about Jim Terkel, she would have told her. "Maybe she's worried about her grades," she suggested. "You know she's been having a lot of trouble in sociology, and Aldridge practically threatened her with a pink slip."

"I don't think that's it at all. She was happy as a clam a couple of weeks ago. Something went wrong on her last date with Terkel." She lowered her voice and added, "She was really upset that night. She came storming into the room, called him a creep, and said she never wanted me to mention his name again."

Betty tried to look properly shocked. "It's really too bad."

"It certainly is," Agatha said feelingly. "But if Jim doesn't realize what a terrific girl she is—well, then, it's his loss." She gathered her books together and smiled warmly at Betty. "Who's new in your life? You must have somebody you're keeping under wraps. I haven't seen you at any of the mixers lately."

"There's no one in particular," Betty said, embarrassed. She didn't want to admit that she hadn't had a date since she arrived at Hastings.

"Well, you're smart to play the field." Agatha stood up. "Of course, I'm the wrong person to give advice. I'm strictly a one-man woman. Since I got engaged to Bud, I don't even want to look at other guys."

"I guess that's what they mean by a one-and-only," Betty said solemnly. "It's too bad Bud is so far away."

"It's awful being separated from him," Agatha agreed, "but there's always the reunion to look forward to." She winked at Betty. "I'll see you later about the party."

Watching Agatha walk toward the reference room, Betty felt a pang of envy. How lucky Agatha was to be engaged, to know that the person she loved loved her. Betty thought sadly of Mitch Goudy. Would she spend the rest of her life writing letters to him in her diary? Maybe someday she would get up the nerve to tell him her true feelings. . . .

Alone in her room, Cynthia was trying unsuccessfully to memorize a list of Prussian kings.

When the phone rang at four-thirty, she was surprised to hear Sandi's voice. "Want some company for dinner? My perm just canceled on me."

"I've got to work tonight," Cynthia glanced at her watch. "I do the dinner shift on Sunday."

"Oh yeah, I forgot." Sandi paused. "That's okay, I'll grab something on the way home."

There was a wistful note in her sister's voice that moved Cynthia to say, "The food's lousy, but if you want to come eat in the cafeteria with me, you can."

"I'd like that," Sandi's voice brightened. "It sure beats going back to South Street. If I eat any more Chinese food, I'm going to turn into an egg roll. I'll be over as soon as I can catch a bus."

After Cynthia hung up, she remembered the Sunday night menu and smiled. The special was chop suey.

"I'm still glad I came," Sandi said, looking at the murky stew in front of her. She was perched on a wooden stool at the far end of the cafeteria kitchen, watching Cynthia methodically peel and chop vegetables.

"At least dessert is good tonight. Ice cream with chocolate or butterscotch sauce. I'm having peppermint ice cream and chocolate sauce. Boston is an ice-cream lover's heaven." She sighed happily.

"I think I'll save my appetite for that." Sandi grinned. "Is there an ashtray handy? So this is where you spend—what, ten or fifteen hours a week?"

"About twenty. And sorry, but you can't smoke in the kitchen."

Sandi sighed and put the pack away. "I don't know how you do it, honey," she said admiringly. "I know the classes here must be tough."

"They are. I already told Mom and Dad not to expect to see my name on the honor roll this semester."

"I'm sure they know you're doing the best you can." Sandi took out a stick of gum. "I finally talked to Mom last night. About me and Neil, I mean."

"What did she say?"

"She was furious. She said not to tell Dad yet." Sandi noticed one of the cafeteria workers looking at her curiously and lowered her voice. "Because he'd probably shoot Neil on sight."

"Huh! That's too good for him. Every time I think of that bastard—" Cynthia brought the knife down on the cutting board with a violent whack.

"Look, these things happen," Sandi said mildly. "Who knows why he's the way is? Maybe there were just so many things happening in his life that he couldn't handle them. He changed a lot once he was out of work and started drinking, Cynthia. Honest. He never used to be like this."

"That doesn't excuse what he did, and you know it, Sandi. He may have you conned into thinking that he's not to blame, but I know better. How come he decided to beat you up instead of picking on one of his drinking buddies? Did you ever think of that? Because he figured you couldn't do much about it, that's why."

"He has a terrible temper—"

"Sure, and he always managed to keep it under control when he was around guys his own size," Cynthia observed. "He beat you up because he could get away with it, Sandi. Period. Besides, if you go back to him, it'll be like giving him permission."

"That's what Mom said, that I'd be asking for it. I've already decided to see a lawyer tomorrow. And I'm hoping it won't cost an arm and a leg—after all, there's nothing to divide."

"You did the right thing, Sandi." Cynthia untied her apron and wiped the chopping block. "I'm all finished here. Why don't we grab some dessert and coffee and sit in the dining room?"

"I don't believe it! Cynthia and her sister! They're right over there by the coffee machine." Adelle Maris's lips curved in a thin smile as she jabbed Susan McMahon in the arm.

"That's nice," Leslie Shaeffer remarked from the end of the table. "I know Cynthia's very close to her family."

"She has a very close family," Susan hooted. "Wouldn't you say so, Adelle?"

"Definitely." Adelle grinned at Leslie's blank look. "Cynthia's sister is a working girl," she explained.

"A working girl?" Cathy Thomas looked up in surprise. "What's so funny about that?"

Adelle stared at her. "You really don't get it, do you?"

"No, I don't," Cathy protested. "I heard Cynthia telling someone that she had a really tough job in Boston. She's on her feet all day."

"On her back is more like it," Susan sneered. "I guess I've got to be the one to spell it out, gang." She paused dramatically and looked around the long wooden table. "Cynthia Woyzek's sister is a hooker."

"That's ridiculous," Leslie Shaeffer gasped.

"Oh no, it's true," Adelle said smoothly. "I heard her scheduling clients right in the lobby of the Carillon Hotel. I was there for the Sigma Chi dance last weekend."

"Do you think Cynthia knows all about it?" Cathy Thomas asked in amazement.

"Who can tell?" Adelle shrugged. "I wouldn't be surprised, actually."

Leslie Shaeffer shook her head sadly. "She looks like such a nice girl. It makes you wonder what the world is coming to, doesn't it?"

No one answered her. Leslie sipped her coffee and sneaked another glance at Sandi out of the corner of her eye. A prostitute, right here in the dining room!

"Tell me something, Cynthia." Sandi

leaned forward. "Do I have my head on backward, or what? There are some girls a couple of tables over who can't take their eyes off me."

"Who?" Cynthia turned just in time to see Leslie Shaeffer turn her head away. Leslie's ears were bright red.

"Actually, there are three of them. The one with the horn rims and the cute brunette and especially that one I met in your room last week."

"Adelle Maris." Cynthia stared hard at Adelle, who gave her a cheery wave. Susan McMahon, sitting next to Adelle, looked self-conscious and defiant. What's their problem? Cynthia thought angrily.

"I told you I had a bad feeling about Adelle, honey," Sandi went on. "I hope you don't have much to do with her."

"Zero contact," Cynthia said. "We don't have any classes together, and we certainly don't hang out much. You're worrying for nothing, sis."

"I hope so. It would be nice if you could make some good friends here. I always figured that would be the best part of living in a dorm." Sandi stirred her coffee and smiled. "Or are the guys keeping you so busy you don't have time for all that?"

"There's nobody special in my life, believe me."

"You never did tell me what happened with the one who took you out to dinner."

"Oh, him. We just decided to go our

separate ways. It was no big deal for either of us." Cynthia avoided Sandi's eyes.

"You seemed pretty excited about him at first." Sandi lit her cigarette at last and sighed deeply.

"He wasn't really my type," Cynthia hedged, "but I didn't realize it until I got to know him better."

She was relieved when Sandi started talking about their younger brother Danny. Cynthia asked lots of questions about Danny so Sandi wouldn't return to the previous subject.

Later that night, as she was climbing the stairs to the second floor, the warm molasses voice of Agatha Mitchell stopped Cynthia dead in her tracks.

"Are you sure Cynthia doesn't suspect anything?" Agatha was saying. "It sure would be a shame if someone spilled the beans."

"She doesn't have the slightest idea," Betty Berke answered.

"Good," Agatha said approvingly. "Then she'll be the last to know."

The conspirators giggled. Cynthia heard a door open and close. She stood for a moment, stunned, wondering what to do. *The last to know what?*

When she got to the head of the stairs, the hallway was empty. She walked slowly to her room, more baffled than ever.

Chapter 13

"You're going to come see me race this Sunday, aren't you? Just think, it's the first race of my entire career!" Jacqui Orsini's brown eyes were dancing with excitement as she and Cynthia crossed the campus, ducking their heads to avoid the blustery wind that whipped through the main quad.

"Since when is race-car driving your career?" Cynthia demanded. "I thought you were all set to be a concert violinist."

"Well, I want to do that, too. Music will always be very important to me, but racing is different. It's exciting and challenging—"

"And dangerous," Cynthia interjected.

"Not as dangerous as you think." Jacqui looked so earnest that Cynthia almost burst out laughing. "Do you know that you actually have a greater chance of slipping in the bathtub than getting hurt in a stock-car race?"

"I'll remember that next time I take a bath."

"Please do!" Jacqui laughed.

Cynthia glanced at Jacqui, trying to imagine her behind the wheel of a race car. The shy young girl who had seemed destined for the concert stage now seemed ready to take on the world.

"Isn't it funny," Jacqui said thoughtfully. "Until I met Pete I never would have had the nerve to try anything like this. And you know what the best part is? I'm really good at it." She turned up the collar on her camel-hair coat and sighed happily. "It's crazy how one person can turn your life around."

When Jacqui headed for the biology building a few minutes later, Cynthia made a sharp left and headed down a narrow path toward humanities. Suddenly her heart skipped a beat. There, no more than fifteen feet ahead of her, was Jim Terkel.

Luckily he had his back to her, or he would have heard the sharp exclamation that she couldn't stifle. He was walking rapidly down the path, deep in conversation with Mitch Goudy.

Cynthia slowed her steps, praying they wouldn't turn around and spot her. She didn't want to see Jim again, didn't want to have to smile and say hello, didn't want to pretend that everything was okay. Nothing was okay, she thought unhappily. Jim Terkel was, as Jacqui said, someone who could turn your life around.

It was going to take a long time to get over him.

* * *

"How did you do?" Agatha Mitchell was asking Betty Berke.

Betty dumped a fistful of bills on Agatha's floral bedspread and gave a triumphant grin. "I haven't counted, but it looks close to thirty. I didn't ask Adelle or Susan. I figured they wouldn't give anyway, and it'd be just like them to let the cat out of the bag."

"Good thinking. Who *needs* 'em?"

"How can people be like that?" Betty plopped on the bed and watched as Agatha emptied her tan leather Gucci bag and started counting the money. "You collected a lot more than I did!" she exclaimed.

"I told everybody ten was the minimum donation." Agatha grinned.

"No wonder you're a business major!"

"You're still sure Cynthia doesn't suspect anything?"

"I'm positive," Betty declared. "She's going to have the shock of her life when we burst into her room one minute after midnight." Betty looked at the money. "Shall I take some of this to buy cake?"

"No," Agatha said firmly, "this is all for Cynthia. I'll buy the refreshments." She tapped the untidy heap of bills. "All this is going for a gift certificate at Carpelia."

"Carpelia?" Betty gulped. "I never even go window-shopping there. Isn't it kind of expensive?"

"Of course it's expensive. That's why I picked it."

"Happy birthday!" One minute Cynthia was sound asleep, and the next she was sitting up in bed. The room was flooded with light. Girls in bathrobes were standing all around.

"Hey, give her a chance to wake up, you guys," Agatha pleaded. She carefully placed a giant chocolate cake on the desk and walked over to the bed. "Happy birthday, roomy!" She gave Cynthia a hug, then stood back, ginning from ear to ear. "I surely didn't think a whole dormful of girls could keep a secret, but it looks like we did it. You didn't suspect a thing, did you?"

"No, I didn't," Cynthia said, slowly coming back to life. "Betty, were you in on this?" She spotted her friend uncorking a wine bottle in front of a stack of paper cups.

"Of course." Betty grinned impishly. "But the real credit goes to Agatha. If she hadn't spotted the birthday card from Sandi, we never would have known this was the day."

"Actually, it's tomorrow." Cynthia laughed.

"No, it's today. We waited until one minute after midnight. Grab some wine, everybody, because we're going to make a toast to the birthday girl." Agatha waited until Betty had finished pouring the wine and then raised her cup in a salute. "To Cynthia, a great roommate and a terrific friend."

"To Cynthia," everyone chorused, downing their drinks.

Someone flipped on the stereo and the pulsing beat of Prince's latest album filled the room.

"Hey, you better turn that down," Cynthia said. "Karen Jacobs will have a fit. You know how she is about noise after midnight."

"I resent that," Karen called out from the back of the crowd.

"Sorry, Karen, I didn't see you."

"That's okay. Dorm advisers are supposed to be invisible."

Cynthia took a swig of wine and looked around the room, still in a state of shock. The girls had actually thrown a surprise party for her! Nan Deluca, Leslie Shaeffer, Jacqui Orsini, and a dozen or so others . . . they *liked* her. She couldn't get over it. She had always been a loner.

A few minutes later some of the girls drifted into the common room to eat the cake and Agatha sat down on Cynthia's bed next to her. "So how does it feel to be eighteen?"

"I don't know yet. It sounds a lot older than seventeen, doesn't it?"

"It sounds really grown up," Betty Berke said seriously. "I remember how excited I was when I turned eighteen this summer. All of a sudden you can do everything—you can vote, you can get married without your parents' consent—" She broke off and flushed when she caught Cynthia smiling. "Not that I'm planning to run off and get married," she stammered.

"How about you, Agatha?" Jacqui Orsini inquired. "Are you going to wait it out till your senior year?"

"Well, Bud is champing at the bit"—Agatha laughed—"but I'm doing my best to hold him off till then—three whole years!"

"Three years? That's a lot of cold showers," Daphne Riesling said wryly.

"Oh Lordy, I almost forgot something." Agatha jumped to her feet. "Hey, gang, turn down the music and pile back in here. It's time to give Cynthia her present." She handed Cynthia a small white envelope. "This is from all of us. Since we didn't know what to get, we thought it would be best to let you pick out something yourself. There's just one rule," she added. "You can't buy anything practical. You have to get something wild and extravagant that you don't really need."

"Like four angora sweaters?" Daphne suggested.

"Okay, so I got carried away last Saturday," Agatha admitted. "Something happens to me when I go to Carpelia. I just can't control myself."

"You gave me a gift certificate for

Carpelia?" Cynthia looked wonderingly at the gold-embossed logo on the envelope. "And it's for"—she looked at the amount and gulped—"a hundred and fifty dollars! I can't take this," she said in a little voice. "It's too much. Way too much."

"Don't be silly," Nan Deluca told her. "With Carpelia prices the way they are, you'll probably end up with a belt and a scarf." She flipped the stereo back on. "Hey, Betty, where's the wine? The party's going to slow down without refills."

Everybody started talking at once. For a moment Cynthia sat alone on her bed looking at the gift certificate. She had never dreamed they liked her that much. For a little while all her problems receded before the glow of really being liked at last.

"I love Boston on Saturdays," Agatha said, squinting against the harsh sunlight that poured over Newbury Street. "And I really love this part of the city, don't you? There must be a mile of boutiques."

"We're going to Carpelia first, aren't we?" Betty Berke asked worriedly. "After all, that's what the trip is for."

"Hey, you guys can hit whatever stores you want," Cynthia piped up. "It's not as if we can all get into the dressing room. I can get by without the whole committee. You want to take off, Agatha?"

"Not on your life," Agatha said emphatically. "The first order of business is to spend that hundred and fifty dollars. And as anyone in Texas can tell you, I'm an expert at spending money."

When they entered the gold and white establishment a few minutes later, Cynthia took one look at the creamy eggshell carpeting and French Provincial furniture and whistled softly. She fingered a silk evening bag and checked the price tag, discreetly hidden inside. "Nan wasn't kidding when she said I'd probably come home with a scarf or a belt, was she?"

"The prices aren't that bad if you know how to shop," Agatha replied. "Did you have something special in mind?" she asked Cynthia.

"Well, not really . . ."

"Good." Agatha looked pleased. "I know just the thing for you. If we plan it right, we can outfit you from head to toe. What are you, about a seven?"

"More like a nine."

"Leave everything to me."

Half an hour later Cynthia emerged with a black jersey cocktail dress, four pairs of textured hose, a pair of black suede pumps, and a beaded evening bag plus a lacy hand-woven evening wrap that Agatha threw in as an extra present from her. "What am I going to wear all this stuff to?" Cynthia wailed. "I should have bought sweaters and jeans or maybe a suit."

"Nothing practical, remember?" Agatha teased. "Donors' terms. Besides, if you suddenly got invited to a dance, you'd need a dress in a hurry."

Cynthia and Betty exchanged a look. Each knew what the other was thinking. Cynthia's chances of going to a dance any time soon were practically zero.

Later that afternoon Betty was in the bathroom getting ready to wash her hair when she heard Daphne Riesling talking to Adelle Maris.

"I noticed you weren't at Cynthia Woyzek's party last night," Daphne said.

"Did you really expect to see me there?" Adelle gave a harsh burst of laughter. "I try to make it a point not to hang out with hookers."

Hookers! Betty froze.

"Hey, c'mon," Daphne said easily, "just seeing Sandi in a hotel doesn't mean anything. Even if Sandi was turning tricks, *Cynthia's* not like that. She's the original straight arrow. I'm sure of it."

"Maybe; maybe not," Adelle answered tartly. "Anyway, the latest word is that Cynthia probably won't be living in the dorm much longer. I heard she and her sister are going to rent a student apartment over on First Street and use it for a cathouse."

"You're kidding!"

"Just telling you what I heard." Adelle's voice was nonchalant.

Betty heard them leave. She stood shivering in the white tile stall, shocked at what she'd just heard. Cynthia's sister, a hooker? That was ridiculous! Why would Adelle say such a terrible thing? And her own room-mate seemed to believe it!

Betty reached for the hot-water knob and suddenly thought of something. If Adelle was lying about this, maybe she'd lied about other things as well. Maybe Jim Terkel had never spread rumors about Cynthia. Maybe it was Adelle that time too.

And Betty had fallen for it! She'd gone running to Cynthia with the news that her boyfriend was a rat. She'd broken up the best relationship her friend had ever had! How could she have been so stupid?

Yanking open the shower door, Betty threw on her terry-cloth robe and wrapped her hair in a towel. The shampoo could wait. Right now she had to straighten out a terrible mistake.

Chapter 14

"Do you think Mario Andretti ever gets butterflies in his stomach before a race?" Jacqui Orsini wiped her sweaty palms on her tan cotton jump suit.

"Of course he does," Agatha yelled. "Anybody in their right mind would." She had to raise her voice to be heard over the roaring engines and squealing tires of two dozen brightly painted cars. It was the third race of the Annual Cambridge Powder Puff Derby, and Jacqui had made a brief foray into the stands to join her friends.

"Look, are you absolutely one hundred percent sure you want to go through with this, Jacqui? There's still time to change your mind." Concerned, Agatha stared at the slim redhead. It was hard to believe that in just a few minutes Jacqui would be strapped in her seat, racing up the track.

"You've asked me that a dozen times," Jacqui said gently. "I told Cynthia the statistics. I'll be completely safe out there."

"Safer than a babe in a bathtub," Cynthia said solemnly.

"You'll never convince me of that," Betty Berke piped up.

"Look at it this way." Jacqui laughed. "If Pete thought there was a chance in the world I'd mess up his precious Trans Am, he wouldn't let me within twenty feet of it. If he has faith in me, why can't you guys?"

"It's not that we don't have faith in you," Agatha said, licking her lips nervously, "it's just that it looks so dangerous. Promise you'll be careful, okay?"

Being careful wasn't the way to win a race, Jacqui thought minutes later as she waited to gun the engine. Even Pete had told her that the whole secret of racing was to take chances, watch for opportunities, and psych out the other drivers whenever possible.

"You've got to feel like you own the track," he'd said. "Act like you're the king of the road. You've got all that power under your feet; don't be afraid to use it."

She didn't feel the least bit afraid, she reflected, resting her hands lightly on the leather-covered steering wheel. She had reviewed all Pete's lessons, and now that it was the moment of truth, she felt calm, almost euphoric.

She felt like a winner.

Suddenly the flag dropped. The orange

Trans Am sprang to life almost of its own accord. Any lingering doubts in her mind had long since disappeared. Jacqui's movements were quick and decisive as she edged away from the outside wall, nudging the car into a more favorable position on the track. The car responded instantly to her slightest touch, as if the two of them, car and driver, were in perfect harmony. It was thrilling.

She knew the capabilities of the car, knew it would hit 60 mph from a standing start in just under four seconds. Seconds— even tenths of seconds—were vital in a race, and she was determined not to hold back.

"I can't look," Agatha Mitchell moaned, one hand covering her eyes. "Did she start okay?"

"Perfect!" Cynthia shouted, her eyes glued to the track. "She's already jumped ahead of that blue Camaro she was worried about. She's moving into fourth place. No, wait—there's a Corvette! He's cutting her off!"

Agatha dropped her hand. "Go, Jacqui, go!"

"Uh, Agatha, I hate to say anything—but she can't hear you."

"Amazing! Did you see the way she cut off that white Chevy?" Betty chortled.

"I can't take much more of this," Agatha groaned. "Tell me when it's over." She started to cover her eyes again, then stopped herself. "My God, is that our little Jacqui? Way out front in that orange car?"

"It sure is!" Cynthia shouted. "Won't it be fantastic if she wins?"

"Lord, just bring her out alive," Agatha begged. "I've aged five years today. I don't have the nerves for this."

"The funny thing is," Cynthia said slowly, "none of us thought Jacqui did either."

"Make the turn, make the turn," Jacqui pleaded softly, fighting the powerful car around the last lap. She was pushing it to the limit, she knew, refusing to touch the brakes, praying the suspension could take the incredible stress.

It did. The car came out of the wrenching turn neatly, clung to the final stretch like epoxy, and roared across the finish line.

Out of the corner of her eye Jacqui saw the checkered flag drop and her heart stopped.

She had won.

Minutes later Pete confirmed the good news. "You're fantastic!" he shouted, enveloping her in a crushing hug. "You're a born racer—I knew it!"

Jacqui scanned the bleachers for her friends. A tide of well-wishers surrounded her. Flashbulbs popped. Someone opened a bottle of champagne, and the fizz shot in the air, splattering everyone. Before she could protest, Jacqui was hoisted on two pairs of strong male shoulders and swept away.

* * *

"Do you think we can get down there to her?" Cynthia looked doubtfully at the throng.

"No way." Agatha shook her head. "It's a madhouse. Why don't we wait and catch up with her back at the dorm? I'll get a bottle of wine and the three of us can celebrate in the room. Okay, Betty?"

"Sure," Betty replied, but her voice was subdued. All afternoon she'd struggled with the problem of what to do about Cynthia and Jim Terkel. She was still miles away from a solution.

Later that afternoon Louisa Fenquist stopped in front of Betty's open door. "You look like that Rodin statue, 'The Thinker,' " Louisa observed.

Betty was sitting on the window seat with her chin cupped in her hand. "I think my brain's stalled." She turned around. "The more I think, the more confused I get."

"Trouble with math again?"

"Oh no, this is a personal problem." Betty slid off the window seat.

"Well, I won't keep you from it." Louisa started down the hall when Betty suddenly said, "Wait a minute, Louisa. Maybe you could help. I mean, if you want to."

"Well, of course I do. You know what they say about two heads being better than one."

Then it all came out. Betty told the whole story about Cynthia and Jim and the part that Adelle had played in their breakup. She also told Louisa about her own crush on Mitch. She just couldn't live without seeing him again.

"Mitch could be the answer to this whole thing," Louisa offered. "After all, he's Jim's friend and fraternity brother—probably the one person in the world that Jim would listen to. All you have to do is go to Mitch and tell him exactly what you told me."

"Oh, but I couldn't," Betty gasped. "He's never even called me. It's clear that he has no desire to see me."

"I doubt that very much," Louisa said gently. "Besides, what do you have to lose? You do want to get Cynthia and Jim back together again, don't you?"

"Yes, of course I do," Betty said feelingly. "If only I hadn't listened to Adelle and her stupid lies—"

"Don't waste your time worrying about that now," Louisa said briskly. "The first thing you have to do is call Mitch and ask him out on a date."

"What?"

"This is the eighties, you know. Women don't have to sit by the phone anymore waiting for the right guy to call."

"I couldn't call him—not in a million years. I'd die!"

"Well, you said you've been writing to him in your diary for weeks. Write him a *real* letter and ask him to go out with you. Come on! Get moving!"

* * *

"This was really a neat idea," Mitch said on the following Saturday night. "I've never had a girl ask me out before."

"I've never asked a guy out before." Betty gulped. "Not for anything."

"I'm glad you made the exception for me." He reached across the red-checked tablecloth and closed his hand over hers. It was dark in Carlo's House of Pizza. Flickering candlelight played over his warm eyes and ruggedly handsome features.

"I wanted to see you again," Betty blurted out, "but I probably would never have gotten my nerve up if it hadn't been for Cynthia."

"Cynthia Woyzek?" He frowned. "That's the girl who dumped Jim Terkel. He was pretty hurt. What does she have to do with this?"

"Everything," Betty said quickly. "And she didn't dump Jim—oh, I know it seems that way, but there's a lot you don't know. When you hear the story, you'll probably think I'm the biggest idiot in the world."

"Maybe, maybe not," he said. "Tell!" He listened silently while Betty tried to explain her part in the misunderstanding.

Betty was close to tears by the time she finished. "You should have seen how happy she was the night they played miniature golf together."

"Yeah, Jim told me about that. He said he couldn't wait to see her again."

They were silent for a moment, each lost in thought. "We have to get them back together, you know," Mitch said finally.

"I've gone over and over it," Betty said miserably, "but I just can't come up with anything."

"I could talk to Jim," Mitch offered. "I could tell him everything you just told me." He gave her hand a squeeze and smiled. "I think they could straighten this out a lot quicker on their own, don't you?" Without waiting for a reply, he suggested, "Why don't I ask Jim to give Cynthia a call tomorrow?"

"No, that won't work. I don't think she'd even talk to him. She's too hurt, even though she won't admit it. I know something that might work, though. The Homecoming dance is next Saturday night, you know."

"You want Jim to ask Cynthia to the dance?"

"No," she said triumphantly, "I want you to ask Cynthia to the dance. All you have to do is get Jim to go to the dance alone, and then we can set them up, get the two of them talking, just like you said. What do you think?"

"I think you're a genius." He grinned. "It's too bad we're in the middle of a pepperoni pizza"—he smiled—"because you really deserve a kiss for that."

She grinned back at him and felt her heart do a funny little flip-flop in her chest.

"The night's still young," she pointed out. "How about it if I take a rain check?"

Everything's working out perfectly, Betty decided the following day. She and Cynthia had just taken their trays with sweet rolls and coffee to a long table by the cafeteria window.

"This is the first time this semester I've actually sat down to eat breakfast on Sunday. Usually I'm too busy serving it," Cynthia said with a rueful smile. "You know something? I think I could learn to like luxury." She took a sip of her steaming coffee and stared at her friend. "Is there something going on that I don't know about? You've got this funny little smile on your face."

"Do I?" Betty murmured. "I guess it's because I heard something interesting last night."

"What's that?" Cynthia said absently, reaching for a Boston *Globe* someone had left on the table.

"I heard that you're going to the Homecoming dance with a Phi Delt."

"What?" Cynthia put down her cup so quickly the coffee sloshed into the saucer. "This is a joke, right?"

"No, it's no joke," Betty assured her. "In fact, I heard it from an impeccable source—your date."

"My date? Now I know you're kidding."

"No, I'm not. He told me he's going to call

you this week to set up the time, and he told me he hopes you're going to wear black, because he's crazy about brown eyes and black dresses."

"And who is this Prince Charming you've dreamed up?"

"I didn't dream him up," Betty protested, "but now that you mention it, he is very charming—"

"Betty—" Cynthia said threateningly.

"It's Mitch Goudy."

For a moment there was dead silence. "Mitch Goudy?" Cynthia finally said. "He's not interested in me. And anyway, he's your . . . I mean, I thought you were madly in love with him."

"I like him a lot," Betty said casually, "but I'm over that crazy crush I had on him. We do see each other, but just as friends. We had dinner together last night, and that's how he happened to tell me he's going to ask you to the Homecoming dance."

"Betty, I told you, he's never shown the slightest interest in me. I don't even know him very well."

"Well, he told me he was going to ask you. We'll just have to wait and see who's right."

"He's in the same fraternity as Jim Terkel. And you know what Jim's saying about me!"

"Honestly, Cynthia Woyzek, you are the most suspicious person I've ever met. Mitch is a really nice guy. Why can't you give him a break and go out with him?"

"Why did he pick me?" Cynthia persisted. "There's dozens of available girls around here."

"Who knows? Maybe he's shy and has a hard time asking for dates."

"Sure."

"Well, I think you're nuts if you don't go. This is the first Homecoming dance of your college life, and you have a brand-new outfit burning a hole in your closet."

"I never expected to wear it."

"Well, you should. Go and have a good time." Betty reached for a sweet roll and smiled. "I can practically guarantee you will."

Chapter 15

"You're sure Betty doesn't mind you going to the dance with Mitch?" Sandi asked in disbelief. "It sounds to me like you're setting yourself up for a whole lot of trouble."

"I can't understand it either," Cynthia admitted, "but Betty was grinning from ear to ear when I told her Mitch called me last night. Whenever I try to pin her down, she just smiles and tells me I'm going to have a terrific time. It doesn't make sense, does it?"

"Not unless Betty's a saint. Talk about being self-sacrificing! I never heard of anybody turning their guy over to another girl without a fight."

"She claims she and Mitch are just friends." Cynthia shivered and stood up. The dorm room was chilly on this dank Saturday afternoon. She started out to hunt for an extra sweater when a light tap on the door stopped her.

"Who's ready for dinner?" Betty Berke

stuck her head in. "Oh, hi, Sandi. I didn't know you were here."

"Just checking up on my kid sister," Sandi joked. "Is it really time for dinner?" She glanced at her watch. "I didn't mean to take up your whole afternoon," she said to Cynthia. "You said you were supposed to go to the library before five."

"That's okay. I'm way ahead in sociology. I'm still in shock—Aldridge actually liked my last paper. He gave me a ninety-two on it, and that brings my average up to a B plus."

Sandi smiled. "Honey, that's great. You didn't tell me about it."

"She probably didn't have time to," Betty said mischievously. "Not when she's got so many exciting things going on in her life. Did she tell you about her date for the Homecoming dance?"

"I told her," Cynthia said. "Sandi thinks all sane college men want to take me out. The ones who see other girls are just consoling themselves."

"A perfectly proper attitude in a sister," Betty said piously, "and possibly even true."

"Thanks for the vote of confidence, anyway." Cynthia smiled.

"I can vouch for Mitch," Betty said simply. She tugged a white wool beret over her copper curls and made a face. "Now, are we going to stand here yakking, or are we going to be the first in line for mock meatballs?''

"Mock meatballs?" Sandi's eyebrows lifted.

"That's the special at the cafeteria tonight. The cook's on a tofu kick," Cynthia explained. "Instead of using meat, he takes these thick slabs of white tofu and—"

"Give me a break." Sandi laughed, reaching for her coat. "I still remember the chop suey. If it's okay with you, I'll settle for a gallon of hot coffee instead."

"Oh God," Adelle Maris said softly to Daphne Riesling, "the gruesome twosome are at it again, and this time they've got your innocent little roommate with them." She laughed hoarsely. "Personally, I don't think Betty Berke would make a very good hooker. She giggles too much."

Following Adelle's gaze, Daphne looked toward the window table that Cynthia and Sandi were sharing with Betty. "Betty says you're way off base on that," Daphne remarked. "She's gotten to know Sandi pretty well, and she claims she's as straight as Cynthia. She's working as a beautician—"

"Oh come on!" Adelle rolled her eyes.

"—in Boston," Daphne finished. She eyed Adelle speculatively. "Where did you say you got your information, anyway?"

"I told you what I saw," Adelle protested. "Sandi was soliciting business right in the lobby of the Carillon. There's no question about it, she's a hooker. I don't know why you won't believe me."

Daphne shrugged. "She just doesn't look the part, that's all."

"Well, maybe not right this minute," Adelle agreed. She smiled nastily. "This is probably her day off. I'm sure she saves her striped eyeshadow and leather miniskirts for . . . working hours." She pushed her tray aside and lit a cigarette. "What *was* that God-awful stuff, anyway? Surely it wasn't meant for human consumption."

"Mock meatballs." Daphne put down her fork and reached for her coffee. "I'm glad I'm on a diet." She sipped her coffee. "Did you know that Cynthia lost ten pounds this semester? She sure looks great. She bought a sexy new dress for the Homecoming dance, and she positively slinks in it."

"Cynthia Woyzek is going to the Homecoming dance?" Adelle sounded outraged.

"Why shouldn't she? Betty said she's going with a Phi Delt."

"You're kidding! Not with—I mean, which one?" Adelle stammered.

"Mitch . . . Mitch Goudy."

"Oh, him." Adelle breathed a sigh of relief. For one awful minute she had thought that Cynthia had managed to snare Jim Terkel for the biggest dance of the year. "A nobody," she said coolly. "It figures."

"You never let up, do you?" Daphne eyed

her table mate. "Why do you always have it in for Cynthia?"

"Maybe I don't like phonies." Adelle pulled on her rabbit-lined Alpine jacket and stood up. "I think Susan and I are the only ones around here who see through her little Mary Sunshine act."

By the time Adelle got back to her room, she was seething at the injustice of it all. Susan was there, sprawled on her bed reading a book.

"Hey," Adelle interrupted, "did anyone call while I was at dinner?"

"You were expecting maybe Billy Joel?"

"Very funny." Adelle walked over to the bed and flipped her roommate's book closed.

"Hey, you lost my place!"

"You'll find it again."

"In *War and Peace*?"

"Seriously, were there any calls?" Adelle demanded, an edge in her voice.

"Seriously? No!"

"Damn." She threw herself down in the easy chair and tried to think. There must be some way of getting Jim Terkel to invite her to the Homecoming dance. He wasn't going with Cynthia, so with any luck he'd be free.

There was some mail on the table. Adelle began sifting through it idly when her eye was caught by a greeting card. "What's this?" The cover showed a solemn-looking character with a forefinger pointed skyward.

"I bought that to send to Steve," Susan said. "Isn't it darling? If that doesn't give him the message, nothing will."

Adelle read the line: "Somebody up there likes you, but I'm down here and ready for action." She liked that line. It certainly wasn't subtle, but maybe it was exactly what Jim Terkel needed to shake him up.

"Steve's been spending all his time studying, and I never get a chance to see him, so—"

"Susan, can I have this?" Adelle broke in. "It's kind of an emergency."

Susan frowned. "Well, I don't know. It's really cute, and I might not be able to find another one."

"Hey, you know that black see-through sweater you like so much—the Oscar de la Renta?" Adelle asked in a wheedling tone. "How would you like to borrow it for your next date with Steve? If you wear that, you won't need the card. He'll know what to do."

Susan smiled. "You've got a deal."

Cynthia and Betty Berke were trying to persuade Sandi to stay in the cafeteria and have another cup of coffee with them.

Sandi hesitated. "I don't know. It's already six-thirty, and I don't want to miss my bus back to town."

"You've got plenty of time," Cynthia pointed out. "You don't have to run off just because I've got to work. Why don't you sit and relax with Betty for a while—and call me tomorrow, okay?" She gave her sister a brief hug and headed for the kitchen.

The minute Cynthia rounded the corner, Betty breathed a sigh of relief. "Thank goodness! I was afraid I wouldn't get a chance to talk to you alone."

"What's up?"

"Gosh, it's all so complicated, I don't know where to start." Leaning across the table, Betty whispered, "Did you notice the girl in the Alpine jacket who walked by the table before—Adelle Maris?"

"I know her, all right," Sandi said grimly. "I met her with Cynthia a couple of times, and she seems like a first-class bitch."

"She is." Betty nodded. "She's had it in for Cynthia ever since school started."

"Cynthia can take care of herself."

"Face-to-face, sure, but that's not Adelle's style. You wouldn't believe the stuff she's been spreading around about Cynthia— about you, too."

"What do you mean? I don't even know her."

"Well, she thinks she knows you. Adelle's been saying that you're a . . . a hooker." Betty choked on the last word, her face flaming.

"What!"

"I know, it's crazy," Betty said hastily, "but that's what she's been telling all the girls. She swears she saw you at the Carillon Hotel one night—"

"I *work* at the Carillon," Sandi interrupted, "as a hairdresser. I go up to the clients' rooms to do their hair, and—this is ridiculous! Why should I have to explain what I do?"

"You shouldn't. You don't—not to most of us. Adelle just wants to make Cynthia look as bad as possible. She's even saying that the two of you are going to rent a place off-campus to do business. And she doesn't mean styling hair."

Sandi's mouth narrowed into a thin line. "What's Adelle's room number?"

"Sandi, I don't think you should—" When she saw the look on Sandi's face, she knew it was useless to argue. "Three twenty-six, but be careful."

"Men are so dense sometimes," Adelle said to Susan McMahon. She had just spent fifteen minutes debating what to write on the card to Jim Terkel. She finally decided to play it cool and wrote, *Hope we can get together again soon. Adelle M.* She liked the last touch—she thought it had a certain woman-of-the-world style to it. "Anyway, it's disgusting. You have to practically throw yourself at them to let them know you're interested."

"Are you talking about anyone in particular?" Susan inquired.

"I mean men in general," Adelle answered curtly.

"You're not still carrying a torch for Jim

Terkel, are you? I thought you gave him up for a lost cause."

"Hah! I never give up," Adelle insisted. "He's getting to be more of a challenge than I thought, though. I can't believe he hasn't asked me out yet. If I didn't know better, I'd think I was losing my touch."

"I don't get it," said Susan. "To listen to you, I'd think you really had the hots for him."

"I don't understand it myself," Adelle confessed. "There's just something about him. First, I thought it was because he seemed so cool. Now . . . well, I don't know what it is."

"The next thing you know, you'll be looking at china and silver patterns like Betty Berke."

"I'm not that far gone yet."

"Good. But I'm keeping you under close observation."

Just then, there was a furious knock at the door.

"Hey, hang on," Adelle said irritably. "You don't have to bash it down." She headed for the door.

An instant later, she was staring into the smoldering eyes of Sandi Woyzek.

Adelle took a step backward, then recovered. "Well, surprise, surprise. The Welcome Wagon lady's here." She glanced over her shoulder at Susan, who burst into giggles.

"You can stuff the jokes." Sandi strode

angrily into the room. "The game's over!"

"What game?" Adelle inquired.

"The game you've been playing with my sister." Sandi looked around the room, then focussed on Adelle. "I suppose you think it's funny to play her for a fool, but you took on the wrong person."

"I don't know what you're talking about. Do you know what she's talking about?" Adelle smiled brightly at Susan.

"Not a clue." Susan ducked her head back into her math book. She couldn't resist peeking over the top, though. From the expression on Sandi's face, this should be a fight to end all fights, she thought happily.

"I understand you've been spreading some lies about me and Cynthia," Sandi said coolly.

"Why should I do that?" Adelle faked a yawn. "I don't even know you. As for Cynthia, let's just say she's not one of my favorite people. As far as I'm concerned, you two don't even exist." She sat down at the desk. Ignoring Sandi, Adelle picked up some papers and began reading.

"You're a damn liar." Sandi swept the papers to the floor. "You've had it in for Cynthia for weeks. You're out to hurt her any way you can. I had your number the minute I met you."

"Who do you think you are, coming in here and carrying on like this?" Adelle demanded. Leaping up, she pulled the door open. "I don't have to put up with this crap. Just get the hell out of here—now!"

Sandi stood very still, her eyes blazing. "I'm not going anywhere until I make sure you've got something straight. Anything you do to Cynthia, you get back from me—twice! You got that?" Sandi took a step closer to Adelle and shoved her lightly on the shoulder. "Maybe Cynthia doesn't know how to handle someone like you, but believe me, sweetie, I do. I've seen your kind before."

"Hey, stop that!" Adelle yelped. "Susan, did you see what she did?" She faced off with Sandi. "You don't frighten me one bit."

Sandi smiled, her face close to Adelle's. "I can frighten you plenty," she snarled. "Just give me a chance." For a moment, it was a standoff, the two poised motionless in the center of the room.

"Sandi, why don't you just go?" Susan snapped her book shut and stood up. "You said you came to say something, and you said it."

"All right." Sandi's eyes never left Adelle's face. "Just so Adelle got the message."

"She got it." Susan stepped between them and gestured to the open door. "Now, take off."

Sandi's eyes locked with Adelle's for a long moment. Then, without saying another word, she turned quickly and left.

"Thanks for the vote of support." Adelle's voice was heavy with sarcasm. "You could have stepped in a little quicker, you know."

Closing the door, Susan stared at her roommate. "I can't believe you, Adelle. You made up all that stuff about Sandi, didn't you?"

"I did not!" Adelle snapped. "She's nuts. Can't you see that? She's absolutely nuts, like her sister."

But Adelle could not keep the quaver from her voice.

Chapter 16

"Maybe this wasn't such a good idea," Cynthia said hesitantly. "What on earth will Sandi say?" She stared at herself in the mirror. Her hair was dripping rust-colored hair dye all over her bathrobe, and her head was covered with dozens of pieces of tinfoil.

"She'll love it," Agatha said. "Now hold still."

"I'm still not sure I want to," Cynthia moaned.

"Don't be silly. We're already over the worst of it. Once I get all the tinfoil in place, I can start painting."

"Well, then hurry up! I've been sitting still so long my feet have gone to sleep."

Agatha picked up a tiny wire brush. "This is the tricky part. You just paint the top layer—that's what gives you that streaky day-at-the-beach look. Don't worry, I've done this a zillion times."

Betty studied the "True Blonde Frost and Paint Kit" and said doubtfully, "I think you'll have to settle for an afternoon at the beach. In case you don't know it, guys, the Homecoming dance starts in exactly two hours and forty-eight minutes."

"Is it that late already?" Agatha began furiously dabbing peroxide on Cynthia's foil-wrapped hair. "Don't wiggle."

"Well, hurry up. I can't go to the dance looking like a walking gum wrapper."

"All this yak is slowing me down," Agatha said ominously. "Now for heaven's sake, hold still." She turned to Betty for support. "She's going to look sensational, wouldn't you say?"

"You'll be the foxiest babe there, Cynthia." Betty eased herself off the window seat and stretched. "I've got to do my nails and hair, so I'll catch you later, okay? I can't wait to see you in that black dress."

"Are you going to the dance? I thought—" Agatha began, and caught herself. "I mean, who are you going with? You never said you had a date."

"Oh, I don't," Betty replied breezily. "I'm going as a single. After all, this is the eighties. See you later."

"I've got to ask you something," Agatha said, shortly after Betty left. "Have you figured out what she's up to?"

"You mean why Mitch Goudy invited me to the dance?" Cynthia shrugged. "She must have put him up to it, but I don't have a clue why. If Betty says she and Mitch are just good friends, I guess it must be the truth."

"I find that hard to believe. I don't think I've ever seen anyone more in love than Betty was. You don't just turn sisterly after something like that."

"What do you think—too much?" Adelle arranged her breasts in her slinky silk top and gave a little shimmy to jiggle them.

"Not if you like the grapefruit look," Susan retorted.

"Fun-nee."

"What's the big deal, anyway? I thought you said Scott Hammer was nothing special."

"He's okay." Adelle inspected a long, perfectly manicured nail. "He's a hunk, though. With that black hair and those smoky eyes. Those could lead you right to the sack."

"Can he walk and talk?"

"Who cares, as long as he looks terrific and can dance?"

Susan leered suggestively. "It sounds like he can offer a little more than that."

"Oh, we'll have to wait and see what happens," Adelle said vaguely. She started to douse herself with musk oil, then stopped, remembering Cynthia's crack. Maybe it was a little strong. She reached for a bottle of Shalimar instead.

"Shalimar, huh? Now I know you're not

expecting much out of this guy." Susan always maintained there was a direct correlation between the perfume a girl wore and the quality of her sex life. "You wear Shalimar when you go out to dinner with your father," she hooted.

"I don't want to kill Scott on the first date," Adelle said. "Who knows? If everything works out tonight, he might develop into a steady thing."

"Yeah? Doesn't sound to me like you've got the hots for him. Not like you did for what's his name, Jim, er . . . ?"

"Terkel," Adelle finished for her, her mouth suddenly dry. Damn! He hadn't answered the funny card she sent last week. And when Friday had rolled around and she still didn't have a date for the Homecoming dance, she'd pounced on the first decent-looking guy who crossed her path—Scott Hammer, a handsome jock with bedroom eyes. He had been checking out the reference stacks in the library and it was the work of a moment to wangle an invitation from him. He'd made it clear that she could pretty well have anything else she was in the mood for.

Adelle sighed as she added a smudge of violet eye shadow, wishing she could summon some enthusiasm for the evening. Scott was a very attractive guy. She certainly wouldn't be embarrassed to be seen with him. Then what was wrong?

She knew exactly what was wrong. Scott

Hammer wasn't Jim Terkel. But then, who was?

When Cynthia was called to the telephone an hour later, she was positive that it was Mitch Goudy, breaking their date. Don't make a big deal out of it. Act like it doesn't matter, she warned herself. Except that it was impossible not to be disappointed. She was already dressed. Her newly created gleaming streaked hair looked ravishing, and she knew she was in top form.

"Hello," she said slowly, prepared to face the worst.

"Honey, I know you're busy getting ready to go out, but I just had to talk to you." Sandi's voice, low and excited, hummed across the wires.

First relief, than a hint of annoyance. What now? "That's okay, I'm ready on time. What's up?"

"I lucked into a great job, that's what. No more working for peanuts at the shop, no more Carillon Hotel. From now on I work nine to five. And dig this: I'm a teacher!" Her voice was quavery with excitement.

"A teacher?"

"At the Middlesex Cosmetology School. I answered an ad they put in today's paper, and they told me to come in for an interview right away. I don't believe it—but they hired me!"

"Sandi, that's terrific." Cynthia felt a rush of pride. No matter how tough things were, Sandi never gave up. "When do you start?"

"Monday. Which is also moving day. Tips have been terrific, and I found this great little apartment that overlooks the river."

Cynthia listened as Sandi prattled on happily about her job, her salary, and her co-workers.

"So you can see, things are finally working out."

"I'm glad," Cynthia said warmly. "You deserve it."

There was a pause, and then Sandi cleared her throat and said a little nervously, "Speaking of people getting what they deserve, I'm seeing a lawyer on Monday. He said I shouldn't have any trouble getting a divorce." She gave an embarrassed laugh. "So I'm losing a husband and gaining a job, all in the same day."

"You're doing the right thing, Sandi."

"I know. It's still hard, though. I guess I'll always have a soft spot in my heart for him."

"It's better than having a soft spot in your head from him beating you up."

"You know something? You're absolutely right."

They laughed and Sandi asked about Cynthia's upcoming evening with Mitch Goudy.

"Are you nervous? It's a big thing, your first Homecoming dance."

"I don't feel too bad yet, but I'll probably fall apart once he gets here."

"Just stay cool. Remember, he's the lucky one. He's taking my kid sister to the Homecoming dance."

"I'll be sure to tell him that," Cynthia said dryly, "just in case he forgets."

"You look fantastic," Mitch said softly to Cynthia an hour later. When he closed his arms around her for a slow dance, she rested her cheek lightly against his. "You should always wear black." He touched a shimmering strand that had escaped from her barrette.

"Thanks. You don't look so bad yourself."

"Really?" he said in mock surprise. "Must be the lighting in here. Or I should say, the lack of lighting. The candles don't do much, do they?"

"I like it this way." Cynthia looked around Donnelly Auditorium, amazed at the transformation that had taken place in just twenty-four hours. A portable parquet dance floor stretched between two giant buffet tables decorated with yellow roses and shimmering candelabra. The band was playing mellow hits from the sixties. Through an open door, Cynthia could see out onto a white marble terrace.

"If you're happy, I'm happy." Mitch smiled.

He was a terrific dancer. Cynthia caught

a glimpse of her reflection as he guided her
past a long mirrored wall. Her cheeks were
flushed with excitement and the black
dress from Carpelia fit like a dream.

She looked sensational, but one thing was
driving her crazy. What was she doing here
with Mitch Goudy? She was about to ask
him exactly why he had invited her when
suddenly she saw something a few yards
away that made her knees turn to jelly.

Jim Terkel and Adelle Maris were dancing cheek to cheek, swaying sensuously to
the music like they were the only two
people in the room. Adelle, braless, in a thin
silk top, wearing skintight cocktail pants,
was flashing her tiger eyes, pressing the
whole length of her voluptuous body
against her partner.

Suddenly Adelle looked up and stared
right at Cynthia, an insolent smile playing
about her lips. For a long, agonizing
moment their eyes locked and held. Then
Adelle molded herself back against Jim,
wrapped her arms around his neck, and
wriggled contentedly.

Cynthia stepped on Mitch's foot and
stumbled. "Hey, watch it," he murmured.

"Sorry. I thought I saw someone I knew,"
she stammered. She forced a bright smile
although her evening was ruined.

The moment Adelle had spotted Jim
Terkel in the foyer, she'd made up a hasty

excuse and dumped Scott Hammer on a delighted freshman from Stevens Hall.

"Do me a favor and dance with Marcia a few times, okay, honey? She's a really sweet girl, and there's someone here I've just got to talk to."

Scott hadn't liked that one bit, but Adelle didn't have time to worry. She was already on her way to pick up Jim.

It was an easy matter to drag Jim onto the dance floor. The tough part was trying to get him to talk. He stayed remarkably closemouthed even though she was flirting like a maniac, practically rubbing up against him.

"It must be karma," she said coyly.

"Karma?"

"You and me tonight. Don't you think it's funny we both ended up at the same place at the same time?"

"I guess so." He stared at a point somewhere over her left ear. If she didn't know better, she'd swear he was bored.

"Did you . . . uh . . . get my card?"

"I got the message," he said dryly.

"Cute, huh?" She heard herself laugh a little nervously.

"Cute."

They were silent for a minute, and then Adelle tried again. "I had kind of hoped you might call me and ask me out." She turned the full force of her emerald eyes on him and tried a little pout. "It's no fun if I always have to bump into you accidentally."

"Oh, it's never an accident meeting you, Adelle." She looked up, puzzled, and he smiled coldly. "More like a disaster."

"What are you talking about?" she demanded, forgetting the movie-star voice.

"I'm talking about what you did to Cynthia Woyzek and me."

"Oh, Cynthia's never liked me," Adelle purred. "I don't know if it's a jealousy thing or what. . . ." She stared at him, trying to read his expression.

"Cynthia's jealous of you?" he said, his voice heavy with sarcasm.

She couldn't back down now. What had he heard? "Yes, right from the start. So if she's told you something about me . . . well, just remember, there's two sides to every story." She smiled and began rubbing the back of his neck. When Jim remained silent, Adelle felt encouraged. "Cynthia has a lot of problems. . . ."

"Don't give me that crap."

"What?" She was stunned.

"You heard me, Adelle, I'm on to you; don't you get it? I know exactly what you've done to Cynthia. You've had it in for her since she got to Hastings. You've spread lies about her. You managed to break us up. . . ." He shook his head disgustedly. "You even told people her sister was a hooker. Don't you stop at anything?"

Adelle was about to shoot back a reply

when she noticed Cynthia Woyzek staring at them. Instantly, she knew what she had to do.

"I never stop at anything to get what I want," she said silkily. She nestled contentedly in his arms. "And I think deep down you really want me, even though you won't admit it."

She brushed his ear lightly with her lips. Cynthia was still watching spellbound. Jim tried to pull back, but Adelle had her arms wound tight around his neck. "It's no good to fight it." She pouted. "Can't you just go with the feeling?"

"You stupid bitch," he said softly. "What makes you think I want anything to do with you?"

Adelle pulled back and smiled. From the corner of her eye, she saw that Cynthia was safely looking the other way.

"It doesn't matter now, Jim Terkel," she said softly. "I couldn't care less about you, either."

Chapter 17

Cynthia had a cold, sick feeling in the pit of her stomach. No matter how hard she tried, she couldn't erase the picture of Jim and Adelle together on the dance floor. The sight of Adelle playfully nuzzling Jim Terkel's ear was captured like a freeze-frame shot—she knew it would be burned in her memory forever.

"Feel like something to eat?" Mitch's low voice broke into her thoughts. "Maybe we should hit the buffet table before the piranhas strike."

"Sure, why not?" Cynthia summoned a smile.

They were busily filling their plates when Betty Berke homed in on them, a vision in pale green silk.

"Hi, guys." She was sipping a glass of white wine and she was very much alone. "Are you having fun?" Her eyes twinkled with amusement and her lips twitched as if she had just heard the world's funniest joke. *What was going on?*

"We sure are," Mitch said heartily. "Cynthia's a wonderful dancer." He put an arm around her shoulders.

"You're the dancer," Cynthia insisted. "All I had to do was follow."

"I always like a woman who knows her place," someone said smoothly. This was followed by a burst of rich, masculine laughter. Cynthia turned in surprise.

It was Terence Malley, the Phi Delt from Grosse Pointe who had snubbed her at the frat party.

"It's been a long time, hasn't it?" He smiled ingratiatingly. He'd grown a silly beard—a tiny vandyke that made him look goatish—and Cynthia nearly giggled.

Terence turned to Mitch. "Hey man, how goes it?"

His eyes briefly swept over Betty as Mitch introduced her. Not his type, he decided at first glance. Now the other one, she was something else. He struggled to remember her name. Candy? Cindy? He was going to make a stab at it when the little redhead spoke up.

"It's a great band, isn't it?" She stared at the dance floor wistfully. That gave him the opening he needed.

"It sure is," he agreed. "And I bet . . . Cindy here is a great dancer." He grinned at her.

"It's Cynthia," came back the frosty reply.

"That's what I said—Cindy." He snapped

his fingers and flashed the famous Malley smile again. "I never forget a name. Or a face like yours, honey."

"Elephants never do," she returned.

Mitch grinned and Terence managed a weak smile.

Embarrassed, Betty jumped in again. "Ooh, I love your tan," she gushed. "Where did you get it?"

"Oh, I was down in the Caymans over Thanksgiving," he said casually. Actually he'd spent a solid week under the lamps at a Boston tanning salon, but there was no sense in saying so. "They have nude beaches there, and you can get an overall tan." He leered at Cynthia. "No tan lines. You want to take a peek?"

"I'm afraid not," she said sweetly. "I never cared for English muffins."

"Huh?"

"English muffins," she said in a bored voice. "Toasted buns."

As Mitch and Betty howled, Terence scowled, then recovered. "Ah yes . . ." He winked broadly. "Toasted buns . . . and a woman with a silver tongue. Would you care to take a little spin on the dance floor with me, my dear?" He offered his arm with a mock bow. W.C. Fields always cracked them up. He did it perfectly.

"Humphrey Bogart," Cynthia said smoothly, ignoring his proffered arm.

"What?" Terence glared at her and Betty giggled.

"Isn't that who you're doing—Humphrey Bogart?" Cynthia's eyes were wide with innocence.

"Try again," Mitch urged. "Terence prides himself on his impersonations."

Cynthia frowned and pretended to think. "Well, if it's not Humphrey Bogart, it's got to be James Cagney . . . or maybe Rodney Dangerfield."

"Very funny," Terence huffed. "Look, I'll see you around," he said curtly, turning away to stalk across the floor. He'd only gone a few feet when a shout from Cynthia made him turn in surprise.

"Rich Little!" she yelled triumphantly. Several heads turned in his direction, and after a moment of stunned surprise, Terence ducked into the crowd. He could see that Mitch, Cynthia, and the redhead were all doubled up, laughing their brains out.

"I've never seen Cynthia talk to anyone that way before," Betty said. She was torn between shock and admiration.

"He had it coming." Cynthia sipped her drink. "Conceited creep."

Mitch cringed in mock terror. "Remind me to never get on the wrong side of you. You've got a wicked tongue."

A few minutes later, Betty was swept away by a freshman from Stearns Hall. Mitch and Cynthia found themselves on the dance floor once more.

She caught him looking at his watch and teased him about it. "Bored already?"

"No, I . . . I was just thinking that I have to hunt down Peter Barnes tonight."

"Peter Barnes?"

"He's the chairman of the entertainment committee. I sold some tickets for him at the Phi Delt house, and I need to turn in the money." Mitch patted his pocket. "I don't like to carry around all this cash." He guided her toward the wide-open doors that led to the terrace.

A rush of cool night air hit them and Cynthia shivered. "He's outside?"

"No, I just changed my mind. Why don't we get a breath of fresh air." Mitch guided her toward a marble railing overlooking the garden. "That smoke really gets to me." He breathed deeply and smiled. "This is much better, isn't it?"

"I guess so." Cynthia stared out at the inky blackness and wished she had her coat. Mitch was certainly acting strange.

"Hey, Peter! There's my man." Mitch peered at the crowded dance floor inside. "Cynthia, wait for me right here, okay? I'll just be a second."

"Mitch—"

"Don't move an inch," he ordered, "or I'll never be able to find you again. I'll be right back." Then he was gone.

"Crazy." She shivered. Why did she have to wait out here, half frozen? She started to walk slowly along the marble terrace when a familiar voice, low and insistent, made her jump.

"Cynthia?"

She spun around, then turned quickly away. It was Jim Terkel.

"We need to talk."

"No, we don't." He took a step closer. She looked desperately for an escape. There must be some way off this terrace. "We have nothing to say to each other," she blurted out.

"You're wrong, Cynthia," he said in a voice that could make an iceberg melt. "We should have had all this out weeks ago. It would have saved us both a lot of unhappiness."

"I thought we *had* it out," Cynthia replied. "You made it pretty clear what you thought of me. A one-night stand. A weekender. I don't mind what you may think of me privately, but you didn't have to spread rotten rumors." She was dangerously close to tears. Seeing him again had touched a nerve inside her, and all the old hurt came rolling back.

"I didn't start any rumors, Cynthia. That was Adelle's work."

"Is there a difference?" Cynthia asked sarcastically. "I mean, you and Adelle were so *close.*" She lifted an eyebrow. "Shouldn't you be getting back to her? She must be getting lonely right about now."

"I'm not with Adelle tonight."

"I saw you with her," she said venomously.

Jim shrugged. "She asked me for a dance.

A big mistake. It gave me a chance to tell her exactly what I thought of her." Cynthia looked so puzzled he took a chance and put his hands lightly on her waist. "Don't you understand? It was Adelle. She told your friend Betty that I was spreading rumors about you. She knew loyal old Betty would go running straight to you with the rumor. And that's what happened, isn't it?"

Cynthia nodded. "Betty said it was all over school. I guess it never occurred to me to ask where she heard it." She looked up at him, her heart pounding.

"It was so easy," he said bitterly. "One conversation, and Adelle managed to break up the best thing that's ever happened to me."

"I . . . I was the best thing that ever happened to you?"

"You still are." He pulled her close; she let her arms slide around his neck. It felt so wonderful. . . . "If you still feel the same way, maybe we can take up where we left off," he said huskily.

"Do you think it's working?" Betty asked Mitch Goudy anxiously. "They've been out there for an awfully long time. Either they've fallen in love or they've frozen to death."

"Maybe both," Mitch responded. The band was playing an early Stones song, and he was enjoying himself. He looked at Betty fondly. "You know, we really owe Adelle one."

"Adelle? That's a laugh."

He nodded. "It sure is—on her. Just think, if everything had gone smoothly with Cynthia and Jim, you probably never would have asked me out for pizza last week. . . ."

"And we wouldn't be dancing together right this minute," Betty said, looking up at him adoringly.

"That's right." He brushed his lips across her cheek. "And think what we would have been missing."

"I don't want to think about it," Betty whispered. She knew exactly what she would have missed: the love of her life. But now that she and Mitch were finally together, where would it lead?

"This is the start of something fantastic, you know." He smiled as if reading her thoughts. "For us, I mean."

"Is it?" she said hopefully. "Because I wondered . . ."

"Wonder no more." He pulled her toward a dark corner of the dance floor. He kissed her on the lips. Suddenly, she couldn't possibly remember what she was supposed to be worried about.

"Well, was the dance everything you hoped it would be?" Jacqui asked Betty the next day. Cynthia and Agatha looked up expectantly, awaiting Betty's reply. The four of them were assembled in Cynthia's room, sharing two dozen assorted doughnuts.

"Everything and more," Betty said softly. She could feel herself blushing up to her hairline just thinking about Mitch Goudy. But she didn't care. She'd been on a permanent high ever since Mitch whispered the magic words, *I love you.*

"What's this I hear about you and Cynthia trading dates last night?" Jacqui looked from one to the other.

Cynthia and Betty exchanged a look and then burst out laughing. "That wasn't exactly the way it happened," Betty explained. "You see, I arranged for Cynthia to go to the dance with Mitch so I could get her back together with Jim, and—"

"And Mitch made sure Jim went alone, but then I saw him dancing with Adelle . . ." Cynthia looked at Jacqui's puzzled expression and grinned. "It's kind of a long story."

"But anyway, 'All's well that ends well,' " Agatha piped up. She added sugar to four coffee mugs and set them down carefully on the desk. "Everybody's happy now."

"How about you, Jacqui?" Cynthia inquired. "Did you have a good time with Pete?"

"The best. But today's going to be even better. We're installing a brand-new chrome-plated exhaust system in the Trans Am. Wait till you see it; it looks like a silver lightning bolt running down each side, kind of like the Batmobile—"

"I can just picture it," Agatha said wryly. "What I can't picture is you with your head under the hood of a car. I can see wanting to drive, but why on earth do you have to go in for getting grimy?"

"Pete says that the more you understand the car, the better you drive. I have to learn about the machine so I can take care of it and so I know what I can expect from it. He also says that if you don't understand the car, you're a lot likelier to get killed."

"Sounds delightful. And you're always telling me how safe it is. Besides, look at your fingernails—you'll never keep your manicure decent."

The other girls laughed.

"Hey, guess what?" Jacqui exclaimed when the laughter died down. "There's a road race over in South Boston, and I won the right to drive in it. This time it'll be against guys!"

"Here we go again," Agatha moaned.

"Hey, no sweat. Everyone says the first time is the worst."

Later, when Betty and Jacqui had left, Cynthia said cautiously, "Agatha, something's bugging you, right? You've been so quiet I figured you must be worried about Jacqui."

"I am, but there's something else on my mind." She stood up and stretched, then gathered her blue wool bathrobe tightly around her. "Bud's coming to see me." Her eyes met Cynthia's. "For the weekend."

"Oh." Cynthia paused. "Look, Agatha, if you'd like me to stay with Sandi for a couple of days, it's no problem. . . ." Her voice trailed off, but Agatha didn't answer. A long minute passed.

"I don't know," Agatha said, biting her lip. "I just can't make up my mind about it."

"You've never . . ."

"No, never." Agatha shook her head. "Not with Bud, not with anyone." She laughed nervously. "I'm not sure I want to break my record now."

"But you're engaged," Cynthia said hesitantly. She was afraid to say too much. She had no idea what she would do in the same circumstances. "What's stopping you?"

"Maybe I'm afraid of losing him. . . . Maybe I'm afraid it will change things. I don't know," Agatha said helplessly. She brushed her tangled blond hair out of her eyes and looked at Cynthia thoughtfully. "There've been a lot of other women in his life, you know."

"He's a football star. I guess that goes with the territory, doesn't it?"

Agatha nodded. "Besides being six-two and gorgeous. Anyway, he's had plenty of women—he's even been engaged to some of them—but they've all had a short shelf life, never lasted more than a month or two. So when I met him, I knew I'd have to be on my toes if I wanted to outlast the competition."

"What did you do?"

"Well, I just followed my mother's advice." Agatha grinned. "I acted very mysterious, I played hard to get . . . and I never gave in."

"Except now you're tempted."

"Now I'm tempted. And I know he expects it."

Cynthia sipped her coffee and looked at her friend. "Things do get complicated, don't they?"

"They sure do. Have you heard about Mary Anne Duffy? She's leaving school today."

Cynthia nodded. "The word going around is that she's pregnant. Take a lesson. Be prepared. If you don't need it, you don't have to use it."

They sat silent, lost in thought, until Agatha jumped up, grinning. "Well, I'm never going to settle anything sitting here brooding. What time are we supposed to meet Sandi for that movie?"

Cynthia glanced at her watch. "One-thirty."

"Give me ten minutes to hit the shower and then we'll take off."

"Good, because I want to get back early. I'm meeting Jim for dinner tonight." Cynthia felt a rush of excitement just thinking about him. Last night had been so perfect, so special. They danced every dance and then walked slowly back to the dorm with their arms wrapped around each other. Jim told her they were going to have a wonderful future together, and she was finally ready to believe him.

"Well, I'm glad things are working out for everybody else," Agatha said ruefully. "You've got Jim . . ."

"And Betty's got Mitch."

"Sandi's got a job . . ."

"Jacqui's got a race."

"And I've got . . ." Agatha looked at Cynthia helplessly.

"A big problem," Cynthia interjected. "But like you said, you're not going to solve it by standing around moping, so, please, hit the shower. You've got exactly seven minutes left." She grinned when Agatha grabbed a towel and made a fast exit.

Somehow Agatha would work things out with Bud; she was sure of it. If they really loved each other, they would stay together whether Agatha slept with him or not.

And as for Betty . . . the glow on her face told the world that she and Mitch had something special.

Cynthia wandered over to the window and stared at the Hastings campus, now so familiar to her. She stood quietly for a few minutes, watching a young couple carve their initials on a tree. Would she and Jim Terkel ever do anything that corny?

Probably. She smiled, remembering what he had said to her on the steps of Windsor Hall.

"Tonight is just the beginning. . . ."